WITHIN THESE WALLS

Miss K

Felicity Douglas

Within These Walls

Futura Publications Limited

A Futura Book

First published in Great Britain in 1975
simultaneously by Arthur Barker Limited
and Futura Publications Limited

This book is based on the scripts by David Butler and Felicity Douglas for the London Weekend Television series WITHIN THESE WALLS

ISBN 0 8600 71626
Printed in Great Britain by
Hazell Watson & Viney Ltd
Aylesbury, Bucks

Futura Publications Limited
49 Poland Street,
London W1A 2LG

CHAPTER ONE

Faye Boswell walked down the stairs of her pleasant house in Highgate, trying to ignore the butterflies in her stomach. She had been appointed Governor of Stone Park Prison, that grim Victorian building on the north side of London, and she started work that morning.

She had been surprised and delighted when she heard that her application had been accepted. Surprised, because her liberal ideas were well known from the books on prison reform which she had written, and they might have stood against her. Delighted, because her position as Governor would give her the opportunity to initiate many reforms which she felt to be long overdue.

Not that it would be easy. She was sure that she would encounter opposition from the existing staff when they learnt of the changes she meant to make. 'Tact, my girl, tact and plenty of it. That's what will be needed,' she said to herself, as she reached the kitchen door, pushed it open and went in.

On the table lay a scrawled note: 'Don't wake me. Got in late. Paul,' and as an afterthought, 'Good luck with your ghastly job, Ma.'

So he had remembered she was starting today! Faye poured herself a cup of coffee and took it across to the breakfast bar, thinking of Paul as she did so. Maddening, unpredictable, at times worrying – but, providing he got through the hazardous years at university, he would be all right.

And Virginia? If she had lived she would have been twenty-three by now, a young woman, perhaps even a mother herself.

She had been a beautiful and loveable child. On her tenth birthday her parents had been watching her riding, so proudly, on her new bicycle. Then, without warning, without reason, a car had shot out of a side road and killed her instantly while Paul, who had raced ahead, pedalled happily on, shouting to a sister who was no longer there.

Afterwards they had sent Paul away for a year to live with his cousins in Australia for the sake of their company, while Faye, in her grief, turned to work as a solace. She returned to her former job in an Approved School. She also wrote three books, which were to become definitive works on the treatment of young offenders. Her ideas were roundly attacked in some quarters, but later proved to be prophetic. Now her career had reached a new peak in her appointment at Stone Park Prison.

Outside, a door slammed and a moment later her husband came into the room. He was a tall, pleasant looking man, whose expense-account luncheons were reflected in his waist-line. He and Faye had met at Cambridge, where they saw each other constantly, but later drifted apart. When she qualified she went to teach in a secondary school in Poplar, where the poverty of the pre-war East End had a profound effect on her social conscience. During the war, Faye joined the A.T.S. She became an officer and discovered she had a natural flair for administration and organisation.

After the war, she became interested in juvenile delinquency and took a refresher course in social science. She applied for and got a post as Assistant Superintendent of an approved school for girls in Yorkshire.

In 1948 she met Bill again. He had become disillusioned with teaching, had trained as an architect and was now working for a firm of Consulting Engineers.

They fell very much in love and married the following year. Virginia was born a year later and Faye gave up her job to devote herself to her family. They were happy though financially strained.

Now, in their early fifties, they were both of them successful in their own fields. Bill was away a great deal, overseeing the construction of factories and offices all over the world. Faye used to say that this was one of the reasons why her middle-aged marriage was such a success, since she never had time to tire of Bill, and he did not feel neglected by her devotion to her job.

He put a small package in front of her plate.

'I got the car out for you,' he said. 'Butterflies?'

'A bit. You do think I'm doing the right thing?'

'Taking the job? How often must I tell you? I'm sure of it. Now open your parcel.'

Faye did so. It was a buttonhole – a white camelia.

'I thought it would look good on that dark green suit of yours; and it does.'

Faye smiled at him, glad that he could not read her thoughts. Dear Bill. How could she arrive for her first day at Stone Park dressed as if she were going to a wedding?

'There's a pin with it,' said Bill anxiously.

She pinned it on her lapel. 'Thank you, and bless you. I must go now. I want to have a little time in hand my first day. I'll try not to be too late tonight.'

'Yes. You do that very thing.'

Taking her bag, she kissed the top of his head, as he opened the *Financial Times*, and became instantly absorbed in it. At the door she met Mrs Burton who had just arrived.

'I'm off now, Mrs B.'

'All right, Mrs Boswell. I'll see to everything; and if you're kept late just ring me, and I'll be round to see to Mr Boswell.'

Rather unwillingly she added, 'Good luck.'

She did not entirely approve of Faye's new job, though, as her son had remarked only last night, 'knowing a bigwig in the nick might come in useful if young Florrie got up to her tricks in the supermarket again.'

As Faye got into her car, she took off her buttonhole and put it in the glove locker. A pity she could not wear it, as it looked well on her suit, but, in view of the drab uniform of the prisoners, it seemed almost insulting to look too spruce.

In fact, one of the first reforms which she hoped to make was to allow the inmates – as she thought of the prisoners – to wear their own clothes, instead of the grey skirts and cardigans, much washed and shrunk, with which they had to be content. How could a woman keep her self-respect in prison, if the first thing that happened to her was the removal of her own clothes and therefore, to a great extent, of her own personality?

As she drove down Highgate Hill, her thoughts were centred on the day ahead. She had already met the senior members of her staff at a sherry party given by the outgoing Governor; and she knew that she was bound to encounter resentment from many of them. The previous Governor, a somewhat conservative woman, who had held the post for many years, had been universally popular.

'But thank heaven,' she thought, 'at least my Deputy is a new broom too.'

Charles Radley, newly appointed Deputy Governor (he had taken up his duties the month before), was also something of an innovation. There had never before been a male Deputy under a woman Governor in a woman's prison. The Home Office had considered it was a worth while experiment and decided to make it under a new Governor, who would not be influenced by past attitudes.

Faye knew that Charles Radley's ideas, like her own, were fairly liberal, so she hoped to find an ally in him. They had talked briefly at the party and had lunched together a few days later, to get acquainted.

Radley was a good-looking man of thirty-nine, a former Assistant Governor at Cricklewood, one of the bigger men's prisons. He was, in a way, more experienced than Faye, having been fifteen years in the prison service. Faye got the impression that he felt this appointment was crucial to his career and that his future prospects would depend on his success at Stone Park. She hoped he would not be over protective to her, highlighting her own inexperience. But he seemed a nice man and she felt hopeful that they would be able to work together.

The rest of the faces at the party had merged into a blurred background. Only two stood out – Miss Parrish and Mrs Armitage.

Martha Parrish, Assistant Governor in charge of South Wing, was a spinster in her early forties. Not obviously an appealing woman owing to her brusque manner, yet she had real beauty, with her high cheek bones and dark deep set eyes. Faye had been told in confidence that Martha Parrish had expected to become Deputy Governor and had been deeply distressed when she was passed over.

Mrs Armitage, the Chief Prison Officer, was a tall woman in her middle forties, who gave an impression of immense strength, both physical and mental, attributes which she would surely need in her job, possibly one of the toughest in the whole prison. She did not smile often and seemed to lack a sense of humour, 'which,' Faye reflected, 'is a pity; for if ever one were needed, it is in this place.' For by now the short journey was over and she had arrived at Stone Park.

Turning in through the tall outer gateway, she made her way to the Car Park and the space marked 'Governor'. Then, uttering a little prayer to whatever gods looked after untried prison governors, she locked the car door and walked towards the inner gateway, with its heavy forbidding doors.

From his window, one of the few in the prison which looked on to the outer courtyard, Peter Mayes, the senior prison doctor, looked down at her with interest. So this was the broom who was expected to sweep the prison clean. She was certainly an attractive woman, with her authoritative walk and her soft ash grey hair; but from that distance he could not see the twinkle in her eye, which was one of Faye's strongest characteristics.

Dr Mayes had read her books and knew of her liberal views. He knew too that many of the prison staff were not viewing her appointment with any pleasure. He did not envy her the first few weeks.

By now Faye had reached the gateway. There was a small door within the great door, and a bell at the side marked 'Visitors'.

'There should be another, marked "Prisoners",' thought Faye. By now she was so nervous that she would not have been surprised if the door had been opened by the Frog Footman himself.

She rang the bell and almost at once the door was opened by the uniformed gatekeeper.

'Good morning, madam,' he said.

'Good morning. I'm Mrs Boswell, the new Governor.'

'Yes, madam. Of course. Will you sign please?'

'Certainly,' and Faye put her signature in the gate book, in which the names of every person entering or leaving the prison are recorded each day.

Penny Halewood, a quiet girl who was to act as Faye's secretary, stepped forward. She and Faye walked along the passage of depressing dirty yellow tiles and into the main hall. Once inside the prison the noise seemed overwhelming – loud women's voices, with an occasional curse, raucous laughter, a shouted order, and the clatter of the cleaning parties' pails. And over it all that indefinable prison smell.

As the Governor and her companion approached the staircase leading to her office, she heard a sudden commotion behind her. She turned. A party of women, in their drab clothes, were on cleaning fatigue. One of them had trodden on the hand of another who was scrubbing the floor on her hands and knees. There was a scream of rage, a spate of gutter language and a pail of dirty water was flung over the offender. Two prison officers who had been gossiping by the gate hurried forward and, with some adroitness, separated the two shrieking women before too much damage to eyes or hair had been done. The other three women watched avidly hoping for something more to break the boring morning routine. As Faye watched,

Mrs Armitage appeared, as if from nowhere. She had heard the scream from her office. She spoke with great authority.

'What's all this now? Break it up Marilyn. You, Susan, mop up that water.'

She blew on a whistle and two more screws came hurrying up. There was by now instant silence.

'Take these two women to their cells and lock them in. See that Alice gets a change of clothes; she's soaked. Get back to work you others – you'll have to hurry.'

Alice, the drenched prisoner, dared to speak. 'But Chief, I didn't throw it, I . . .'

But the Chief was having none of this.

'You can explain all this at Disciplinary tomorrow. Take them up,' and turning to the other three women who were by now looking scared, 'Get on with your work. Violet, get that pail refilled.'

Muttering, the women went back to work.

Mrs Armitage turned to Faye.

'Good morning, madam. I'd heard you'd arrived.'

'That was quick.'

'News travels fast in this place. I'm sorry about this, (she indicated the wet floor) on your first morning.'

'I suppose it often happens.'

'Constantly. They've not much control.'

'I think it was really a mistake,' said Faye.

'A mistake, madam?'

'Not the soaking – the treading on the hand.'

'I see.' Mrs Armitage did not sound pleased.

'What I mean is—' Faye felt a perfect fool and wished that her sense of fairness had not let her start this argument so soon after she arrived. She was aware that Penny Halewood was listening and no doubt the officers and prisoners. But having started this, she must finish it off.

'I don't think she did it on purpose.'

Mrs Armitage smiled in a rather superior way. 'Don't worry, madam. It won't hurt the girl to cool off for a bit.'

Faye did not agree, but felt that at this stage in the proceedings it was too soon to say so.

At the foot of the stairs which led up to her office, Faye paused and spoke again to the Chief Officer.

'I rang Mr Radley yesterday and asked if he would take Disciplinary and Governors requests today.'

'He told me madam. He has taken them several times this past month.'

'Good. That will give me more time to go round the prison. When you have finished with Disciplinary, perhaps you'd come round with me?'

'I've aranged for Miss Flaxton, that's one of our Principal Officers, to stand in for me today so that I could do so.'

'Good. Then come to my office in about an hour.'

As Faye climbed the stairs, she reflected that Mrs Armitage was a fine disciplinarian: whether she was entirely fair was another matter. 'But,' she thought, 'I must take things quietly and not rush them.' And repeating to herself the advice of the morning, 'Take it quietly and use tact,' Faye went into her office. Her first day as Governor had begun.

CHAPTER TWO

Half an hour later the telephone rang in Dr Mayes' office. It was Penny. Mrs Boswell would be glad if he would go to her office at eleven o'clock for a cup of coffee.

'I'd be delighted,' he said, and meant it.

Over the whole prison the same message was going out – to the Deputy Governor, Administrative Officer, Assistant Governors in charge of the Wings, Welfare Officers, Hospital Sister, all senior staff. Faye had decided to meet them at the earliest possible moment and begin to take their measure; and what better way to do it than over a cup of coffee – and perhaps some of those exotic biscuits which Bill had brought from Istanbul last week? In fact, Faye herself found them rather disgusting, but at least they would be different. And so would the coffee. Faye, who was something of an expert on coffee, had brought in some of her own, which would make a change from the normal prison brew.

Meanwhile, she and Mrs Armitage were going round the prison together.

Stone Park had been built in 1870 in a part of London which was then a prosperous and respectable suburb. In order not to offend the susceptibilities of the residents by planting an obvious prison in their midst, the façade had been designed as a copy of a medieval castle. But behind this impressive front there was just another gloomy Victorian gaol; and so it still was on the day when Faye Boswell took over as Governor.

Their inspection started from the Centre. From there, anyone could survey all the floors of all the wings; and there the Chief Officer had her glass partitioned office. There, too, stood the round, highly polished table on which were kept the various order books and also, perhaps incongruously, a large vase, always full of fresh flowers, beautifully arranged.

As Faye entered the Centre, and Mrs Armitage re-locked the doors behind them, another group of prisoners, on cleaning fatigue and carrying mops, brushes and pails, turned to watch them. One of them, a handsome but bitter looking woman, gave Faye a sycophantic smile.

'Good morning, madam,' she said.

'Good morning.' Faye smiled briefly and passed on.

Lily Hever opened her mouth to speak again, determined to get in well with the new Governor, but before she could say anything, Mrs Armitage had pounced.

'Get on with your work, Lily,' she snapped and followed Faye, to unlock the gates of South Wing.

Lily looked after them with a scowl.

'Bitch!' she muttered to herself, just loud enough for Mrs Armitage not to hear. 'Doesn't want me to talk to the new Madam. Sod her. I'll put in to see the Governor soon. She can't stop that, can she?'

Lily turned to another of the working party.

'See who that is, Norah? It's the new boss. Ever so smart, isn't she?'

Norah, young, pale and bewildered, was not really interested; but she was too frightened of Lily Hever to say so.

'Yes,' she said nervously, 'Lovely.'

'Who was that?' Faye asked, as soon as she and the Chief Officer were out of earshot.

'Lily Hever, She's a bit of a nuisance.'

'In what way?'

'Making trouble: complaining: upsetting people.'

'What's she in for?'

'Fraud, madam. Three years.'

By now they had climbed the spiral staircase to the top storey of the South Wing. Faye stopped and looked down into the deep well, with the wire mesh stretched across it.

'I suppose you're used to this,' she said.

'To what, madam?'

'To these wings. The catwalks, the wire netting.'

Mrs Armitage shrugged. 'That's the way prisons are built, isn't it? I take it for granted. I don't notice it any more.'

'I suppose so. It depresses me. There's something barbaric about it. Depressing for the staff and degrading for the prisoners.'

As she spoke, Faye gave an involuntary shiver. The Chief noticed this and smiled rather grimly.

'That's a matter of opinion, madam. But you must admit it's practical. From the Centre I can see every floor of every wing. So can my officers.'

'Yes, there is that,' said Faye.

'And anyway this is the way it is, and there's nothing anyone can do about it.'

'I wonder,' Faye replied.

Mrs Armitage looked at her, puzzled. Faye decided not to say any more for the moment. It was only her first morning, and there was no point in rushing things.

And so the tour continued, punctuated by the endless clanking of keys, as every gate was unlocked and locked again.

Faye noticed that many of the prisoners were very young, nearly as young as her charges in the Approved Schools where she had worked. She found this depressing.

The North Wing seemed to be deserted. Most of the inmates were either working or in their cells. But on the ground floor there were two old women gossiping in a corner and a young coloured girl sitting aimlessly on a bench. She was staring at her hands and tears were rolling slowly down her cheeks. She did not seem to notice when Faye paused, then looked a question at the Chief.

'Peggy Abbott, madam. She's just come out of solitary.'

'Hullo, Peggy,' said Faye.

Peggy looked up slowly and nodded, then stared at her hands again. She made no reply.

'Why aren't you working?' asked Faye.

After a moment Peggy answered in a low voice:

'Not been given no work, lady.'

As Faye nodded and moved on, Janet Harker, the Assistant Governor in charge of this wing, came out of her office – a converted cell at the end of the row – and moved to meet them.

'Good morning, Miss Harker,' said Faye and went into the office.

'Good morning, Governor,' said Miss Harker and the Chief followed her in.

Faye looked at Janet a moment, then:

'If you'll forgive such impertinence from a total stranger, you must be one of the youngest Assistant Governors in the service.'

Miss Harker smiled. 'I'm twenty-eight,' she said.

'You certainly don't look it. Does she, Mrs Armitage?'

'No, madam.' The Chief's tone was stiff. She had not approved of this pretty fair-haired young woman's appointment.

'Tell me, Miss Harker,' Faye said, 'why isn't Peggy Abbott working?'

Janet Harker hesitated, then glanced at the Chief, who spoke immediately.

'It was my recommendation, madam. The girl's been in solitary. Only came out yesterday. I thought it better to give her a day or two to adjust.'

'I see.' Faye's voice was thoughtful.

Then she turned to Janet Harker with a smile.

'I must get along. So much to see. But you'll come down to my office for coffee in about an hour?'

'Thanks. I'd love to.'

As she came out of her office, Faye noticed Peggy Abbott still sitting, motionless and staring. She said nothing to Mrs Armitage, but made a mental note to look into this later. She turned to Mrs Armitage:

'I'll see you at coffee,' she said, 'and this afternoon we must continue our inspection. You're being so helpful.' She smiled with such charm that the Chief smiled back briefly: but she thought to herself, 'Her ways aren't my ways; nor ever will be.'

The coffee party made a break for the staff; and the coffee itself came in for much appreciative comment. Faye renewed her acquaintance with most of her staff and met for the first time the Chaplain and the Roman Catholic Priest who divided his time between Stone Park and Cricklewood Prisons.

She also met and liked Dr Mayes, an amusing man with tremendous energy, who flirted happily with any woman he happened to be speaking to, with the exception, Faye noted, of Mrs Armitage and Miss Parrish. Faye noticed these two having a word together and wondered why her ears were not burning. She felt sure that they should have been.

After everyone had gone back to their various duties, she had a long talk with one of the Welfare Officers, Miss Clarke, whom she had asked to stay behind. Miss Clarke was a red-haired woman with an ugly but pleasant face. Faye had met her before, at a lecture she had given on Child Welfare. For a while they had discussed various problems concerning the welfare of the prisoners and arranged to go together to a forthcoming meeting of the Discharged Prisoners Welfare Association, a subject close to Miss Clarke's heart. Then the talk turned to various inmates. Finally, Faye asked her what she knew of the coloured girl, Peggy Abbott.

It was a common enough story, but nonetheless tragic for that. Peggy had been found living in one filthy room with her two children. She had been sentenced to nine months for 'persistent child neglect'. Peggy had only left her native Nigeria when she was fifteen, and her English was limited.

She had married at sixteen and at eighteen had been deserted by her husband and left with the two small children. Miss Clarke felt that her neglect of them came from a total inability to cope. In prison she had been withdrawn and at times violent, when other inmates had taunted her with being a bad mother.

'Are the children in care now?' asked Faye.

'No, they are with her uncle. A very respectable man. The Reverend Henry Atanga. It was he who sent for Peggy hoping she would help his wife in a busy parish. But Peggy met this merchant seaman and married him as soon as the law allowed. Mr Atanga is very bitter about her.'

'Does she see her children?'

'No. He won't allow it. Compassion is not part of his religion. She has had no visitors. No letters.'

'In your opinion, should she have been sent into solitary?'

Miss Clarke smiled. 'My opinion was not asked. So many of these cases need never come here at all. The girl is not bad, only quite ignorant. Of course she did throw a cup of tea in a prison officer's face,' added Miss Clarke dryly. 'And prison discipline must be maintained.'

'Yes. But now she is out, where do you think she should work? You know her; and your suggestion would be helpful.'

'I'd like to see her work in the Maternity Hostel. She misses her own children quite terribly. I'm sure she really loves them and would be thankful if she could have some training.'

'Good idea. I'll speak to Sister, if you would put the suggestion to Miss Harker.'

'Thank you, Mrs Boswell.'

Miss Clarke had been worried over Peggy Abbott and was glad to find that the new Governor seemed to believe in rehabilitation rather than punishment.

Penny Halewood knocked on the door and came in.

'Excuse me, madam, Chef has sent up a message to say the mid-day meal is ready for you to approve.'

For Faye had to go each day and taste and comment

'I'll go down in a few minutes, Penny,' said Faye.

'One of your odder chores,' said Miss Clarke.

'A very necessary one.'

And the two women went their various ways. Faye to the kitchens, where she made the acquaintance of the

Chef, an immense, cheerful man, very popular with the inmates who worked in the kitchens. She then tasted the food, afterwards writing her comments in a book provided.

She lunched with Charles Radley, Dr Mayes and another of the doctors, an attractive young woman who had just qualified. Afterwards she went over the Hospital Wing with the two doctors. Although the medical facilities were all up-to-date and more than adequate, Faye could not help agreeing with Peter Mayes that visually the whole wing was a somewhat depressing place for people who were sick. She determined to allocate part of a forthcoming grant to refurbishing its outward appearance.

She liked Peter Mayes' cheerful manner with the inmates and the way in which he treated them as individuals rather than mere patients.

By seven o'clock that evening, Faye was thinking about leaving. It had been a long day. She had been round the whole prison, visiting every department and inspecting every building, leaving most of the routine work to Charles Radley. She had met all the senior members of her staff and most of the prison officers. She had also had a short session with the psychiatrists and the medical staff, but not, of course, simultaneously; for she knew that they did not mix happily.

On the whole she had been impressed by the sense of duty shown by the prison staff, by their patience and even devotion in a testing job. But she was worried by the rigid outdated views of many of them and of the Chief Officer in particular. Thank heaven that Charles Radley seemed likely to be an ally.

As if on cue, there was a knock on the door and the Deputy Governor came in.

'It's after seven,' he said. 'You've had an eleven-hour day.'

'I don't imagine that's unusual.'

'No. But the first day is more tiring than most.'

Faye rose and opened a cupboard where she kept some personal belongings.

'A glass of sherry?' she said – and poured two glasses.

They sat for a moment in a companionable silence.

'How much ground did you cover today?' asked Charles Radley.

'Literally, a great deal. My legs are aching. Those staircases. Mrs Armitage must have legs of iron.'

'She's an iron sort of woman. But invaluable, in many ways. The women respect her.'

'Or fear her,' said Faye.

'Which comes to the same thing, perhaps.'

'No, it does not!' said Faye, and then smiled at her own vehemence. 'I know you are right about her qualities. But her views are so very reactionary. She nearly had a fit when I said that I hoped to arrange for the inmates to wear their own clothes. Those drab uniforms!'

'They used to be much worse.'

'Two hundred years ago they used to lie on straw with rats running over them,' answered Faye briskly. 'Now, Mr Radley, we must get this straight, from the beginning. I am tiresomely full of reforming zeal and I admit it. The Powers That Be know my views and presumably approve them, or I wouldn't have been appointed. I hope very much for your co-operation. Indeed I need it.'

'You'll get it all right,' answered Radley and smiled. 'Only take my advice and go slow at first. They are a hidebound lot at Stone Park. I've found that already.'

'I'll go slow if I think it's best,' said Faye. 'But you know my views.'

'I've read your books and admire them – even if I haven't totally agreed with them.' And he smiled.

'What a nice man he is,' thought Faye. 'We will disagree without rancour and I am sure he will be totally loyal.'

As if he could read her thoughts, Radley added, 'And, of course, I will back you up in public in whatever unlikely reforms you suggest.'

He got up. 'It's time you went home, Governor, or your husband will have my blood.'

'I must,' said Faye and added, 'I didn't meet your wife properly at that party last week. You must bring her to dinner one evening.' She spoke on impulse and instantly regretted it, for a shadow seemed to fall over Radley's face, and for a moment he looked a sad man. 'Something is wrong with his marriage,' thought Faye and wondered if it would affect his work; and then chided herself for having a one-track mind.

When Faye had left, Charles Radley went into his own office to collect some papers he wanted to take home with him. He wondered, ruefully, what Faye had got that he lacked. For he too had applied for the job of Governor.

The telephone on his desk rang. It was his wife, Beth. Her voice sounded sharp.

'What's happened?' she asked. 'You're late.'

'I said I might be late tonight. I'll be back by half past eight.'

'But the Howards have dropped in. They want us to go to the new film at the Odeon.'

'Why don't you go alone? I don't feel like a film tonight'.

'When do you ever feel like anything except reading reports from your lousy prison? All right. I bloody well will go with them. There's some cold beef in the fridge.'

And before he could answer she had slammed down the receiver.

Poor Beth. How she had changed. Probably his own fault. He must be an unsatisfactory husband, far too absorbed in his work. A pity in a way that they hadn't any children. And in another way, just as well.

Faye lay comfortably on the sofa in her sitting room. On a low table was the remains of her supper which Bill insisted she had on a tray. In the background Beethoven's Pastoral Symphony played softly. Bill sat in an armchair, reading.

It was half past nine and Stone Park seemed a thousand miles away, although she knew that now she would always have one mental foot inside those forbidding doors until the day she left. Even after only one day there she was wondering about the few inmates she had already met personally.

Bill had risen and was handing her a tot of brandy. Every time he came home from abroad he brought some duty-free drink.

'Purely medicinal,' he said, smiling. 'Make you sleep.'

Faye took it, grateful to Bill. She wondered whether Mrs Armitage had such a kind and considerate husband, and somehow doubted it. She did not look like a woman who was used to being cossetted.

Faye smiled at Bill. 'Sorry darling, I didn't ask what sort of day you had.'

'No need to. It's your day that matters – not that I want you to talk about it now – simply relax and go to bed early.'

'I will.' She sipped the brandy. 'Paul's late.'

'He rang. He was going out with Chris.'

'Chris who?'

'None of Paul's friends have surnames.'

'Silly of me. I think he's that immensely tall boy with no chin.'

'Chin or no chin, he's got a boat at Burnham and wants Paul to buy a half share in it.'

'Has he got the money?'

'No. But I have. I'd like to ask your advice. It can't wait, as Chris wants to know tomorrow.'

'You think it would be good for Paul?'

'Don't you? He's showing signs of being keen on sailing and—'

Faye finished the sentence for him. 'He'd have less time left for student politics. I quite agree darling. An excellent idea. I would worry less about Paul if I felt his interests were being channelled elsewhere.'

'So you do worry about him?' said Bill.

'Doesn't any mother with a son at university worry these days? He's been involved in two demonstrations already.'

'He was right about teacher's pay in my opinion.'

'Right or wrong, that's not the point. One simply prays for him not to get involved. Bless you, Bill. I think the idea of the boat is fine, only don't tell him I said so.'

'Why not?'

'At the moment I'm persona non grata with Paul.'

'Why on earth—?'

'I suppose if one is a bit of a rebel, a bit agin authority, it must be galling to have a mother who is part of the Establishment, and one of the grimmer parts at that.'

'But you worked in Approved Schools all the time that Paul was growing up.'

'It's not the same. A Superintendent seems nothing more than a kind of headmistress. Whereas a prison governor has a quite different image. Usually unjustified. Anyhow darling, you buy him that boat. Can I contribute too? You'll be able to go out with him. You always loved sailing when we were younger.'

'It's only a fourteen footer. I've put on a bit of weight since then,' Bill sounded rueful.

'It suits you.' Faye caught back a yawn. 'I must go to bed. I'm dropping.'

'You do that thing.' Bill's arm was round her shoulders. They smiled at each other in the mirror over the fireplace. Two middle-aged people, still attractive to each other and each holding down a job of some importance.

From the photograph on the mantelpiece, the dark eyes of the ten-year-old Virginia regarded them gravely. But they did not notice. At the moment they were only very conscious of each other.

And then Faye spoke rather sadly, 'You know, I think that Paul minded Virginia's death quite enormously. They were such friends.'

'He never said much.'

'Children never mention death. But I think Paul felt it was my fault that car came out of that side road.'

'That is idiotic.'

'I feel guilty all the same. Towards you too. You loved Ginny.'

And they both looked at the photograph in silence. Till Faye said, 'If only I could have had another daughter for you.'

Bill smiled. 'It wasn't for lack of trying. Don't be sad darling. Ginny was happy for the whole of her life. How many of us can say that?'

As they went upstairs together Faye thought of the three hundred odd women in her charge, and how at this moment she would gladly have exchanged her authority, her power, and her handsome salary for one small ten-year-old girl.

CHAPTER THREE

Two days later, Faye had occasion to go to the Maternity Hostel, to see the Sister in charge. The hostel was in fact a fair-sized house, at one time used as staff quarters, and was furnished more like a home than a prison, with curtains and pictures, and bedrooms instead of cells, while the mothers wore their own clothes.

No wonder, Faye thought, that it was a popular place to work. The atmosphere was utterly different from the prison proper.

She finished her business with the Sister, then asked how Peggy Abbott was getting on. Sister looked puzzled.

'She isn't here. I was expecting her, but she didn't arrive.'

Faye frowned, but did not comment, except to say, 'All right. I'll speak to Miss Harker.'

She spent a few minutes talking to the other mothers – nearly all of them very young – and played with some of the babies. She was particularly taken with a curly-haired six-months-old African baby with the smile of an angel and, her mother assured Faye, the temper of a devil.

On her way back Faye thought how the mothers must suffer when at a year old, the babies were sent away, to relations or, more often, into care. That must be the cruellest punishment of all.

Back in the main prison building, she did not go straight to her office, but instead to the North Wing, to see Janet Harker. As she passed throught the Centre she asked Mrs Armitage to join her.

She was not surprised, when she reached the Wing, to see that Peggy was still sitting on a bench, silent and withdrawn. Faye did not speak to her, but went into Janet Harker's office followed by Mrs Armitage, who had a shrewd suspicion why she was wanted and had the light of battle in her eye.

Janet Harker rose. 'Good morning, Governor.'

Faye nodded. Her voice was almost stern.

'Good morning. I have come to find out why Peggy Abbott is still not working.'

'I know. Time to adjust from 'solitary'. Surely that is not necessary?'

Mrs Armitage broke in. 'When a woman is released from solitary, it's as well to keep an eye on her to see if she's learnt her lesson.'

Faye turned to Janet. 'Has she been told where she is going to work?'

'No, Governor.'

'This I do not understand. I arranged with Miss Clarke that she would go to the Maternity Wing, and asked her to speak to you. Did she not do so?'

Janet hesitated. Mrs Armitage was bursting to speak again, but Faye was waiting for Janet to answer.

'Yes, Miss Harker?' she said.

'Well, Governor, there is great competition to work in Maternity. And since Peggy was convicted of persistent child neglect —' she paused.

Faye finished the sentence for her.

'You thought it might cause resentment?'

'Well —' Again Janet hesitated.

'Or someone else convinced you it would?'

Mrs Armitage could bear it no longer. She spoke. 'I advised Miss Harker that other inmates who have behaved as badly as Peggy Abbott will think they have only to pretend remorse in order to be treated softly and sent to a privileged job.'

'I don't agree with you, Chief.' Faye was adamant. 'I can't see that Peggy is pretending to show any signs of remorse. She appears to be totally apathetic, as you can see for yourselves. The Welfare Officer —'

Mrs Armitage muttered something.

'Did you speak, Chief?' asked Faye sweetly.

'No madam.'

'As I was saying, the Welfare Officer suggested that this girl's only chance is to learn how to care for her children properly and it is up to us to give her that chance by sending her to train in the Maternity Wing. Surely you see that?'

'Yes, I'm sorry,' said Janet.

Mrs Armitage was a hard woman, but an honest one. 'I told Miss Harker that, in my opinion, it would undermine discipline.'

'I see. I'm afraid I disagree. I can't say that either of you disobeyed me, because I merely made a suggestion and gave no order. But I don't want my suggestions to be disregarded in future. I would like the girl taken to the Hostel at once by a prison officer.'

'Yes, madam,' Mrs Armitage said, and thought bitterly, 'First round to madam!'

'But first I'll have a word with the girl,' Faye went on. 'Bring her in here, will you?'

After a moment Peggy appeared. How young she looked and how lost, Faye thought, and spoke gently.

'Peggy, we are sending you to work with the babies in Maternity.'

Peggy, in her bewilderment and loneliness, wondered who this nice lady with the silver hair and soft voice could be? Being so withdrawn and speaking English so badly, she had little contact with either officers or fellow prisoners and had very vague ideas of who was in the prison. Nor had there been much effort by anyone else to make contact with her; for, like many slow people, she was often irritating. But now for the first time for weeks, it seemed, someone was talking to her kindly and saying something about babies. Tears came to her huge brown eyes and rolled down her cheeks as she spoke.

'But lady, I'm bad with babies. They said so in the court. And my uncle said . . .'

'Never mind what your uncle said. You are not bad, only untrained. And we are going to train you. At first you'll be doing mostly domestic work – cleaning, helping in the kitchen and so on. But all the time you'll be able to watch the other mothers and the nursing staff; and after a while Sister will start to teach you how to care for children yourself. Go along now, and I'll look in soon to see how you're getting on.'

The Chief took Peggy out, and Faye turned to a somewhat downcast Assistant Governor.

'I'm a bit disappointed,' she said to Janet Harket.

'I'm sorry I let myself be persuaded. It's no excuse. I know, but Mrs Armitage has years of experience and I thought . . .'

'I do understand. But you mustn't let your inexperience undermine your self-confidence,' and Faye smiled at her, and left.

Mrs Armitage and Martha Parrish were having a cup of coffee in the rather cheerless little room where the staff could go when they had time to relax for a few minutes. They were old friends, who had often crossed swords, but who were at present united in their joint disapproval of the new Governor.

'It's all part of the new attitude,' Miss Parrish was saying, 'something we'll have to learn to live with.'

'It will do no good pampering the inmates like this. No good at all. That Abbott girl might have scalded Officer Baines quite badly if the tea had been hot.'

'Fortunately it never is.'

'No thanks to Abbott. And now she is rewarded by being given one of the most popular jobs. In my opinion any inmate who hurts an officer should be made to suffer for it.'

Mrs Armitage spoke with great bitterness. Apart from Martha Parrish, no-one at Stone Park knew that she had reason to hate any violent inmate.

Years ago, when her husband had been a successful prison officer, on the verge of promotion, he had been viciously attacked by a prisoner, who had nearly killed him. He had not died, but was totally incapacitated and in great pain; so much so that he had often begged his wife to put an end to it all.

After a series of operations the pain was reduced, but for a while he had turned from a cheerful husband and father into a cantankerous invalid. Had Mrs Armitage not been a woman of great physical and mental strength, she could not have survived the last fifteen years. As it was, it had been enough to destroy her sense of humour, though never her sense of duty.

If Martha Parrish, after a long day in the prison, felt inclined to grumble, she would look round her neat though lonely flat and think of her friend leaving her job at the prison, only to tackle another one at home.

If only she were not so reserved, and could talk of her troubles! But it was against her nature and this no doubt added to her bitterness over recalcitrant prisoners in general, and Peggy Abbott in particular.

After a pause, Martha ventured to say:

'She did after all get solitary. And I heard she wept constantly in there. So she has been punished.'

'You think I'm being petty?'

'No. Of course I don't. But if the Welfare Officer suggested her going to Maternity . . .'

'The Welfare Officer! Soon there will be more of them than us.'

'I agree there are too many of them,' said Martha Parrish and then, changing the subject, 'They say Mrs Boswell has all sorts of new ideas. Do you know what they are?'

Mrs Armitage answered almost with a snort.

'I know some of them. Prisoners should wear their own clothes. More free association. Longer visiting hours – more educational classes and, (she lowered her voice) this you will not believe – she wants the nets removed and the floors filled in.'

Martha Parrish gasped. 'But think of the extra work that would cause!'

'Exactly. We'd need double the staff and we are short-handed enough as it is.'

There was a short pause while they considered the iniquities of their new Governor. Then Miss Parrish said:

'She seems to be full of excellent theories which couldn't possibly work as things are.'

And Mrs Armitage added:

'I just wonder how much harm will be done before she realises it. I suppose Mr Radley will support her.'

'We must all support her. It's our duty. As for Mr Radley —' there was bitterness in Martha's voice as she spoke, ' – how can a man understand the problems of a woman's prison?'

Mrs Armitage, who knew how much her old friend had counted on becoming Deputy Governor herself gave her arm a consoling pat and poured her another cup of coffee.

The Governor was hearing Disciplinary cases and Prisoners' Applications. The latter was a daily chore. Any prisoners could ask to see her on any pretext and they could not be refused, however trivial the request.

In front of Faye was a large book in which she entered the details of the cases. Mrs Armitage stood at the side of her table, carrying a clip-board.

A sullen, defiant girl, Rita Caine, stood in front of the desk with a uniformed officer on either side of her. She was a dark, gypsyish looking girl. She looked at Faye with some dislike. When Faye spoke her voice was cold.

'I understand you stole a lipstick from one of the cells.'

Rita grunted. 'Shouldn't have left it lying about.'

'That is not the point. Stealing from another inmate is not only despicable, it is also extremely stupid as it makes you very unpopular. I advise you not to do such a thing again. Five days loss of privileges. Take her out.'

Rita was removed muttering to herself.

'Foolish girl,' said Faye.

'No-one likes her much. This won't help,' remarked Mrs Armitage. She had been glad to find that the new Governor, despite her daft ideas about prison reforms was a strong disciplinarian.

'Do you know whose lipstick it was?'

The Chief glanced at he clip-board. 'Yes.'

'Then speak to her. Anyone who leaves personal property lying about in this place, deserves to have it stolen. Who's ncxt?'

Mrs Armitage looked at her clip-board.

'Weekes, Georgina. Application to see the Governor. This is old Mrs Weekes,' she went on, 'a persistent shop-lifter. She's been in before.'

Mrs Weekes came in nervously, bobbing her head towards Faye. She was frail and white-haired, in fact only sixty, but looking much older. She was obviously distressed about something. Faye wished she could ask the poor old dear to sit down. Instead she spoke to her kindly.

'What can I do for you, Mrs Weekes?'

Mrs Weekes gulped, but did not answer.

'Are you in some kind of trouble?' Faye asked.

Mrs Weekes hesitated, then spoke nervously.

'I don't like to keep bothering you, m'm.'

'Don't worry about that. Tell me what it's about.'

'It's – it's me sister, m'm. She said she'd take me in when I'm finished here, now she's a widow.'

'When are you going to be discharged?'

'I don't know, m'm, not exact.'

'Six weeks, madam,' said Mrs Armitage, referring again to her clip-board.

'Not very long,' Faye smiled at the old lady. 'So what's the problem, Mrs Weekes? Don't you want to live with your sister?'

'Oh yes, m'm, I do. But I don't know as she wants me now. I haven't heard nothing, not for ages.'

'Have you written to her?'

'Yes, but I never get no reply now.'

'Does she usually write to you?'

'Oh yes, m'm, regular, up till a month or two ago. It's as if she don't want to know me any more.'

The old woman's mouth quivered, and Faye spoke with deliberate briskness.

'I'm sure it's not that, Mrs Weekes. There may be all sorts of reasons. I'll speak to one of the Welfare Officers and ask her to find out what's happening. We have your sister's address?'

Mrs Armitage intervened, 'We have, madam.'

'So you leave it to me.'

Faye smiled at Mrs Weekes, who summoned up an answering smile of a sort.

'Thank you, m'm,' she said, 'ever so much.'

Mrs Weekes left and Faye made a note to speak to Miss Clarke, at the same time saying,

'Next.'

'Hever, Lily. Application to see the Governor.'

'That's the woman I met on my first day, with the cleaning party?'

'Yes, madam,' said the Chief, 'I'm afraid you'll see a lot of her. It's her way. She books to see someone nearly every day – the doctor – the chaplain – the governor . . .'

'What is the purpose of it?' asked Faye.

'To get off working without losing any pay.'

'Of course,' said Faye, 'I should have known. By the way, Chief, who is that young girl who was with her? They were together again yesterday, watching television, at tea time. Her cell mate?'

To herself Mrs Armitage had to concede that the new Governor didn't miss much.

'That's Norah Williams. She's not her cell mate. She shares with old Mrs Weekes. But Lily always has her hanging around.'

'I see. Let's have Lily in.'

Lily Hever came in, walking with a pronounced limp. She had her story pat. Her feet were giving her agony, terrible. Could she see the chiropodist? It was the day she came to the prison. All this at great length.

Faye listened patiently till Lily had finished.

'I see. But when I saw you earlier today in the Admin. Corridor, you weren't limping.'

Lily was thrown for a moment, but quickly recovered herself.

'You see, madam, it's these shoes. They hurt like hell.'

'Your shoes? If that's the trouble, how could the chiropodist help you? I could, of course, authorise a change of shoes for you. But if you're in such pain you should see the doctor as well.'

'Oh no, I don't want that,' said Lily quickly.

'Why not?'

'Well, he said I was wasting his time.'

'When was this?'

Lily hesitated and the Chief answered for her. 'Last week.'

'And were you?'

Lily did not answer. Faye spoke again.

'You realise, I hope, that if you are deliberately making this up and wasting people's time (not to mention the prison officers who'd have to go with you), it might have to go on your conduct sheet. You wouldn't want that, would you?'

Lily was cornered and she knew it. She put on her most ingratiating smile.

'I'll just grin and bear it.'

Faye was dead-pan. 'You do that.'

And murmuring, 'Thank you, thank you, madam,' Lily backed out, remembering just in time, to limp.

Mrs Armitage was smiling a wry smile.

'We won't see her again in a hurry.'

'I hope not. Lily Hever is a humbug All the same, if she were able to wear her own shoes, she wouldn't be able to make that particular excuse.'

The smile left the Chief's face. This was the sort of 'progressive' talk she didn't want to hear.

Within half an hour all the applications – some like Lily's quite phoney, others moving, some rather funny – had been dealt with. Faye closed the book with a bang.

'By the way, Chief, I wanted to tell you first – no-one else knows except the Deputy.'

'Yes, madam.' The Chief hoped she didn't sound apprehensive. What was coming up now?

'I have heard from the Home Office. They have approved the inmates wearing their own clothes. All of them – not only those on remand.'

Mrs Armitage said nothing, but looked intensely disapproving.

'It will mean a great deal of work and organisation. We must discuss it at the staff meeting this afternoon. But I thought you would like to know first.'

'Thank you, madam. Some of the older inmates won't like it.'

'Probably not. But the vast majority will, and I hope it will do a lot to lighten the prison atmosphere.' Faye rose. 'I'll see you later, Chief.'

One of the Governor's more boring routine chores was going through the mail with the Administrative Officer.

Mr Morton was a dry, spare little man in his fifties. He was still shy of Faye; and in these first weeks she had not been greatly impressed by him. But he had a sharp, practical mind and in his hide-bound way was good at his job. He had been at Stone Park for a long time – over twelve years.

One morning, as they finished working their way through the pile of paper, Mr Morton managed to overcome his shyness enough to volunteer a comment.

'Not quite as much mail as usual today, Mrs Boswell.'

Faye smiled. 'You sound disappointed, Mr Morton.'

'Oh no. Far from it. I don't know how we keep pace with it sometimes. It's never ending.'

And indeed it was. New admissions, remands, letters, requests, complaints, estimates, accounts.

'Never ending,' he repeated. 'I could do with twice as many staff on the clerical side.'

Faye was rueful.

'I'm afraid you're not likely to get any more at the moment. The whole prison service is understaffed.'

'Very true. In fact the Chief Officer was . . .'

He stopped. Perhaps it might not be tactful to mention this. But Faye pressed him to go on.

'She was complaining of the difficulty of keeping the uniformed side up to strength. She feels they'll soon be outnumbered by Welfare Officers and nurses.'

'I'm not sure that that would be such a bad thing.'

Mr Morton was shocked. 'Mrs Boswell!'

'I know the Chief wouldn't agree with me.'

Morton looked at her over the top of his glasses. 'She is not the only one, Governor. Surely our main function is to keep our inmates in custody in disciplined conditions. For that the prison officers are mainly responsible.'

'I believe there is another function in a prison. To give the women a chance to lead more useful lives outside. For that we are all responsible.' Faye spoke with conviction.

'Indeed, yes. But—'

There was a knock on the door and Charles Radley came in.

'I wanted to catch Mr Morton while he was here. Two birds with one stone. It's about the fabric of the South Wing. The Works Officer is worried.'

'Why?' asked Faye.

'It's the oldest part of the building,' said Mr Morton.

'Yes,' answered Radley 'and apparently there's a bit of settlement and one of the outside walls is showing signs of buckling.'

'Is it dangerous?'

'Not at all. But it must be reinforced if we want it to stand for another hundred years.'

'I should think that is the last thing we want.' Faye spoke with some emphasis, and the two men looked at her, surprised. 'I only hope that all these Victorian monstrosities will have disappeared long before then. With any luck there'll be a whole new concept of what a prison should be.'

Mr Morton was prim and disapproving. For him, Stone Park suited its purpose. But Charles Radley smiled at Faye and murmured: 'With luck and several million pounds out of the taxpayers' pocket—'

Mr Morton started to gather together the papers and memos.

'Don't go yet, Mr Morton. This is something which affects you both – all of us in fact. I think you know that I went to a meeting at the Home Office last night? It appears that we are to be allocated a sum of money – about twenty-five thousand.'

'Good heavens,' said Charles Radley and wished he could allocate it.

'I see,' said Mr Morton. His tone implied— 'If *I* had the spending of that money—'

Faye, quite aware of what they were both thinking, went serenely on.

'Since I have only been here for a short time, I want to find out the opinions of my staff before making my decision.'

'Quite.'

'There are so many things,' said Mr Morton.

'Exactly. We must list them in order of priority.'

'Couldn't we have a series of meetings with the various departments, Governor?'

'That would be a good idea,' said Faye. 'Meanwhile perhaps each department could discuss it fully over the next few weeks; and then we'll have a meeting with senior staff and Assistant Governors.'

'That should weed out the more frivolous suggestions,' said Radley.

'I expect we'll get a few of those.'

'I'm quite certain we will,' said Mr Morton dryly.

'So perhaps you would get things moving, Mr Radley?'

And so it was left.

CHAPTER FOUR

A week or two later, Faye was on her way to see Mrs Weekes. It was late afternoon and some of the prisoners were together on the ground floor of the wing, gossiping or watching television. Others were on the upper storeys, standing on the catwalks outside their cells, calling raucously to each other across the well. It was a noisy and uninhibited scene.

As Faye entered the wing and paused to relock the gates, the inmates eyed her curiously, making almost audible comments on her looks and clothes.

Lily Hever and Norah were sitting together on a bench. When Lily saw Faye, she got up and put on her sweetest smile.

'Good afternoon, madam,' she said.

'Hullo, Lily. How's the foot?'

For a moment Lily was nonplussed. Then she remembered the lies she had told the last time she saw Faye, and answered:

'Better, madam, thank you. You were quite right.'

'Good,' and Faye looked at the shy girl with Lily.

'It's Norah, isn't it?'

Norah stared, speechless, and Lily answered for her.

'Yes, madam, Norah. That's right.'

'You share with Mrs Weekes, Norah, don't you?'

Again Norah did not answer, but looked down, embarrassed. Lily nudged her fiercely.

'Answer madam,' she said.

'It's all right, Lily,' Faye said. 'Don't let me disturb you,' and she moved on.

Lily turned to Norah.

'Why didn't you answer?'

'I – I couldn't.'

'Silly clot. I told you. The more you get in with them

the more you get away with. Carrying on like you do, you'll never get nowhere.'

Norah looked miserable, and Lily eyed her, wondering how she could use her to her own ends.

At the open door of Mrs Weekes' cell Faye paused. She made a point of always asking if she could come in. After all, the prisoners had so little privacy, one should respect what they had.

It was a cell of about thirteen feet by seven and painted cream. There were bright chintz curtains, two bunk beds, two wooden washstands, a mirror with a shelf under it, a small table and a chair. Except for the curtains it differed hardly at all from all the other cells. But on the walls, on the hardboard provided, were pinned drawings – good line-drawings and colour sketches, also montages mounted on stiff cardboard.

'Mrs Weekes?' thought Faye. 'Not possible. It must be Norah's work.'

Mrs Weekes, who was a little deaf and had not heard Faye approach, was sitting on the lower bunk, peering at a children's story book with coloured pictures.

'Mrs Weekes,' Faye said, 'may I come in?'

Mrs Weekes gave a little jump.

'Oh, m'm, yes m'm.'

'Don't get up. May I use the chair?' and Faye sat. 'I must say, you've made it very neat and comfortable in here.'

'Oh, it's not me, m'm. It's Norah She's not got much here,' and the old lady tapped her forehead, 'but she's a jewel to share with.'

'And the pictures?'

'She did them too, all of them. She's a wonder. That's my favourite,' and she pointed to a large montage of flowers on the end wall.

'Yes,' said Faye, 'it's most attractive,' and thought to herself 'she might do some really good work.' She turned to Mrs Weekes and said in her most friendly way, 'Miss Clarke, the Welfare Officer, has seen your sister.'

'Is she all right?' Mrs Weekes asked anxiously.

'She is now. But she has been ill and is in hospital.'

'Serious?'

'Not as bad as they feared. But she has had a little stroke and for a while couldn't speak or write.'

'Poor old Jess.' There were tears in her eyes. 'No one to visit her. Wish I could send her some flowers.'

'You can. And perhaps visit her too.'

'Oh thank you, m'am. But I supposc I can forgct about going to live with her.'

'On the contrary. She'll need someone to look after her when she leaves hospital. Do you feel up to it?'

'It would be fine, m'm.'

'You'd have to behave yourself you know.'

'Oh yes, madam. I promise.'

'That would be splendid,' said Faye and rose. As she left she noticed that Lily Hever and Norah were now in the next-door cell and that Lily was combing Norah's hair. As Faye went past, she heard an 'ouch' from the girl, and Lily saying, 'You stupid little tyke you'. But a moment later she had realised that Faye was nearby and had switched to a sweet smile. 'Sorry, darling,' she was saying for Faye's benefit: then she rose.

'Coming to visit us, madam?' she asked. 'That'd be nice.'

Faye passed. Why not? she thought to herself. She had Lily's measure, but she wanted to learn what she was up to with this shy, almost retarded girl.

She went in. Lily's cell was very gay with the drawings on the wall.

'Your's, Lily?'

'No, madam. My friend's. Norah. She's in next door with old Georgie – Mrs Weekes.'

'They're very good, Norah,' said Faye looking at the walls.

Norah nodded, speechless with embarrassment.

'She's shy, madam.'

'So I see.'

There was a pause. Lily was opening her mouth to speak again. But it was Norah whom Faye had wanted to talk to and there seemed very little chance of that. She must try and see the girl alone sometime. Before Lily could speak again, Faye turned.

'I must get along. Your drawings are lovely, Norah. I'm glad your foot is better, Lily.'

As she walked down the iron staircase to her office, she wished she could have been a fly on the wall to hear what Lily was saying to her frightened little friend.

As soon as Faye had left, Lily turned on Norah.

'Why didn't you answer her?'

'Sorry.'

'Sorry's not good enough.'

Norah got up as if to go to the door. Lily pounced and seized her by the wrist.

'Where are you going?'

'To my cell.'

'Why?'

'To get on with my drawing.'

'You're not, you know. Not yet.' She twisted Norah's arm as she spoke

'Lily, you're hurting me.' Norah was white with terror at what Lily would do next.

'Then sit down and listen. That's better. Now, you're getting paid tomorrow aren't you?'

'Yes,' Norah was barely audible.

'D'you know what you're goin' to do with that loot?'

'Yes.'

'What?'

'Buy more colours and paper—'

Lily laughed harshly. 'You're not. You're going to buy fags.'

'You know I don't smoke.'

'But I do, lovey, I do. And if you don't do as I say, I'll tell my friend, Mrs Boswell, you're a nasty little trouble maker – and then you know what she'll do – she'll have you put in solitary. See?'

Norah looked up at Lily, scared out of her wits by her hard, implacable face. Then:—

'I'll get them, Lily,' she said. 'I'll get your fags. Anything you say.'

In the Maternity Hostel, Peggy Abbott was about to be initiated into the mysteries of nursery training. She was watching Sister bathe a six-month-old baby. Sister Chin-Lin was a very pretty Chinese woman, with a soft attractive voice. She spoke perfect English. She dried the baby and held him out to Peggy, who was wearing a big towelling apron. Peggy shrank back.

'Now, Peggy, don't be scared.'

But Peggy was scared. So scared that she drew away.

'I don't know what to do.'

'You have two of your own, so it's time you learnt. Come along. I want you to dress him.'

'You should not trust me. I am bad mother. They said so.'

Sister was firm.

'Come along. Here are his clothes . . .' and she put the baby quite firmly into Peggy's arms. 'Now dress him. I have to go for a few minutes but I'll be back. Take it slowly. Billy's a good boy, he'll be no trouble.'

As Sister left the room, Peggy started to panic. The baby looked at her, puzzled, and then suddenly chuckled. He reminded Peggy of her own son at that age; and for the first time since she came to prison she felt human and no longer an outcast. She held his warm little body close to her for a moment, then started very carefully to dress him.

When Sister returned, the baby was dressed and ready to go out. She thought that this experiment was going to work.

'Tomorrow you can help bath the babies, Peggy.'

'I'd like that.'

'And then I'll show you how to feed them and how to prepare their food.'

'Maybe I'm not so bad after all,' and Peggy actually smiled.

'Maybe not.'

From that moment Peggy did not look back. And the babies loved her.

At the end of that week, after the babies had been tucked up in bed, Peggy went to Sister's office.

'Please, lady,' (to Peggy, everyone in authority was 'lady' regardless of their rank) 'you pleased with me?'

'Yes I am. Why do you ask?'

'My uncle, he say I cannot look after my own babies. But now I am learning?'

'Of course you are.'

'Then – what I do?'

'Why not write to your uncle?'

Peggy was doubtful. Sister realised what was troubling her.

'Ask Miss Harker, she will help you.'

A wide grin spread over Peggy's normally serious face.

'I do that,' she said.

After Peggy had gone, Sister had a word with Janet Harker. And later that evening, after supper, Janet went to Peggy's cell. As a result of that meeting, a letter was written to Mr Atanga, Peggy's uncle.

Janet showed it to Faye before posting it:

'My dear uncle,

I write to you to say that I am having training in the babies home here. I like it and the Sister says I do well. So, when I get out, I will know how to look after my own babies. Before, it was too much. I knew so little but now it will be different.

Please uncle I miss them so much, please may aunt bring them to see me?

I am truly sorry for the trouble I gave you. Not again.

The lady who looks after my Wing help me with this letter since I do not write too good.

Your loving and contrite niece—'

And it was signed in childish capitals 'PEGGY'.

Faye showed it to Miss Clarke who happened to be with her.

'Any luck do you think?'

'I'm not very hopeful. He is a rigid sort of man.'

'Let us send it and hope for the best.'

The letter was posted and Peggy, full of hope, worked harder than ever in the Hostel.

CHAPTER FIVE

Old Georgie Weekes was finding it difficult to sleep. She was due to be discharged, the next day, and for the first time for many years she was going, instead of to a dingy and sparsely furnished room, to her sister's comfortable little house in Stockwell. Whilst her brother-in-law was alive she had not been very welcome, for he was a pompous man, a butcher by trade. But now that her sister was widowed and a semi-invalid at that, Mrs Weekes would live there and look after her and the house. She was beginning to feel for the first time for years, that she was of some importance. The welfare lady had been ever so kind, and had taken her to hospital to see her sister, now on the way to recovery. There wouldn't be any more of that shoplifting nonsense, she thought, now that she had a job to do looking after Violet.

That afternoon she had had a lovely surprise. The dress-making class had clubbed together and bought the material to make her a new dress; for Georgie was popular with the other inmates. She had been given it the day before. She wouldn't disgrace no one in that dress And she wasn't going empty handed neither, for Norah, as they undressed for bed, had said in her shy way that she wanted to give her the big flower picture, 'me favourite' thought Mrs Weekes. They had carefully taken it down and rolled it up, ready to take it out in the morning. She would miss Norah, poor little kid, sure she would. She knew that Lily Hever was up to no good – she wondered if she should say something to Miss Harker – but thought better of it. Everything was peaceful, why stir things up? She did hope that they wouldn't put the girl in with that Lily. The poor kid was in a bad enough state – all nerves she was at the end of the day and she needed somewhere quiet at night.

She turned in her narrow bed, ready now for sleep. It would be funny, she thought drowsily, to sleep in a proper bed again instead of one of them bunk affairs. Not that prison was as bad as it was painted, lovely and warm and the food regular, always plenty to gossip about to the officers She did miss her evening tot though. Well, it was over now.

She became aware that there was muffled sobbing from the bunk above. Fighting back sleep, she spoke.

'What is it, lovey?'

A muffled sentence from Norah.

'I can't hear you. Come down, dearie.'

Norah crouched on the floor, Mrs Weekes' arm round her.

'What is it?'

After a long pause, incoherently, Norah tried to explain. Georgie was her only friend and now she was leaving and what little protection she had against Lily would be gone. 'What should she do? What – should – she – do?'

A gentle snore answered her. Mrs Weekes was not unsympathetic, but it had been a long day and she had fallen into the quick, shallow sleep of the old.

Miserably Norah went back to the top bunk. She must talk to one of the staff, she told herself. And knew that she would never dare. The lady in the prison shop had noticed something. When Norah had gone to spend her money last week she had said: 'Smoking? You don't buy your drawing things any more. It seems a pity, and Lily, who was close behind, had pinched her hard on her upper arm, so hard that she had to bite her lip to stop from crying out.

The worst of it was, she thought miserably, that she was nearly out of paper and pencils now. If she were not able to draw she would go mad, she knew she would. The only way she could stand this place was by drawing, drawing things that she found comforting – and now it looked as though that was going to be taken away from her.

The next morning, Mrs Weekes was waiting for an officer to take her down. The inmates crowded round her, teasing her, patting her on the back, as she came out of her cell, carrying her small suitcase and the rolled up picture, which Norah had given her.

As soon as Lily saw this, she gave a shriek and dashed forward, snatching the picture from the old woman.

'That's mine,' she shouted.

After a moment's shock, Mrs Weekes retaliated. Furious, she snatched the picture back from Lily.

'It's mine, not yours. Norah give it me.'

Norah was pressed against the wall, her hand to her mouth. Mrs Weekes had lost the picture again to Lily, and in retaliation had pulled Lily's cardigan and blouse nearly off. Around them prisoners jeered and murmured. There was a cry from Mrs Weekes, as Lily smacked her hard on the face. The scene was confused and ugly.

Miss Flaxton, Principal Officer on the wing, had been talking to Janet Harker in her office. Now she came forward followed by another officer.

'What's all this? Stop it at once.'

Mrs Weekes, sobbing, let go of Lily. Miss Flaxton held Lily tightly. Janet Harker came out of her office.

'What on earth's happening?' she asked.

'She took me picture,' Mrs Weekes said, 'the one Norah give me to take away.'

Lily was snarling, 'It's not yours, silly old bugger. It's mine. All Norah's paintings are mine.' She swung round on Norah. 'Aren't they?'

Norah did not answer. She was rigid, the rabbit confronted by the snake.

'She took my picture. She took it.' Mrs Weekes' voice rose to a furious squeak.

The picture had by now become unrolled, and Mrs Weekes made a grab at it in a final effort to get it away from Lily, who resisted. Naturally the picture was torn in half. Mrs Weekes gave a shriek of dismay, while Lily swore. They were surrounded by a crowd of women, who were for the most part cursing Lily, though a few were jeering at Mrs Weekes.

Suddenly, as though a tap had been turned off, there was silence. Mrs Armitage had arrived on the scene.

'What's all this?'

A chorus of voices answered her, but she broke in sharply:

'That's enough. The show's over. Break it up.'

Slowly, reluctantly, the prisoners moved back and away. Miss Flaxton released Lily, who muttered to herself as she pulled at and straightened her clothes.

At this moment, unexpectedly, Faye appeared. She had come to the wing for a final, unofficial, word with Mrs Weekes. She looked at the little group for a moment, before she spoke.

'What's happening? And what are you holding, Mrs Weekes?'

Mrs Weekes looked miserably at the torn painting.

'It's all torn now – no good. Norah gave it me for a parting present.'

'Norah never did,' Lily was vehement.

Faye turned to the frightened girl.

'Did you, Norah? I must say it was a nice idea.'

'You never, Norah, did you?'

Norah stared at Lily, at Mrs Weekes, at the Governor and the Chief, all waiting for her answer. Then slowly, unwillingly, Norah betrayed her old friend, Georgie.

'No. I didn't.'

'Norah. How could you ever?' It was a cry of dismay from Mrs Weekes.

The atmosphere was explosive and charged with emotion.

Mrs Armitage looked a question at the Governor, who nodded.

'Take Mrs Weekes to reception, Miss Flaxton,' said the Chief briskly, adding more kindly to the distressed old woman, 'We'll see you before you go.'

Faye added, 'I'm sorry about the picture. I am sure Norah will do you another one. Won't you, Norah?'

But there was no answer and Mrs Weekes was taken away, sniffling audibly.

As soon as she had gone, Lily turned to Faye, in her most sugary way.

'I'm sorry about all that, madam. She shouldn't've done it. Upsetting Norah, poor kid. It's a shame. Now she's gone, do you think Norah could share with me?'

Faye looked at her coldly. 'That's not for me to say, you must ask Miss Harker.'

Lily opened her mouth again but before she could speak, Mrs Armitage had intervened.

'Into your cell, Lily. You can cool down a bit. And, of course, you'll be up before madam in the morning.'

Lily managed to smile in a placatory way to Faye and also to shoot a look of venomous hatred towards the Chief. Quite a feat, thought Faye.

As Lily was led away, Faye turned to Miss Harker.

'Shall we have a word in my office?' she said. 'You too, Chief.' They left. And Norah remained leaning against the wall. She had never been so miserable in her life.

A discussion was taking place in Faye's office as to whether Norah should share with Lily Hever or not.

In Faye's own mind, there was no need for any argument; the idea was unthinkable. But, according to prison protocol, the decision was really for the Assistant Governor of the wing, in this case Janet Harker, and she, to Faye's surprise, did not seem to realise what a scheming creature Lily was, nor how she frightened Norah.

Listening to her, Faye realised that she was bending over backwards to be fair to both inmates.

'She is trying to show how liberal she is,' thought Faye wryly.

Mrs Armitage, however, had no such inhibitions and said so firmly.

'If Miss Harker has no objections to their sharing a cell, I can only say that I'm strongly against it.'

'Why, Chief?' asked Faye.

'There's something wrong there. I'd go even further. I'd move Norah to another wing, split them up as much as possible.'

Janet Harket reacted to this. 'That's quite unnecessary.'

Charles Radley came in and was put in the picture. His advice might help, thought Faye.

'I know you have been concerned about that girl, Chief,' he said.

'I don't see why,' said Janet. 'She and Lily seem devoted to each other.'

'I can't give you a definite reason, but I am uneasy about her,' replied Mrs Armitage.

'So am I,' said Faye.

'She's quiet and absolutely no trouble,' said Janet.

'There is one thing,' said Radley, 'she's taken to spending creature Lily was, nor how she frightened Norah.

'A lot of them do that,' said Janet. 'Cigarettes are a kind of money in the nick. Maybe she's trading them for something.'

'I don't think so. I believe she's giving them to Lily Hever. Some sort of intimidation. I feel something's very wrong. Not that I've ever seen anything and Lily, as you know, is always so plausible.' Mrs Armitage sounded worried.

'Are you sure you aren't making too much of this?' It was Charles Radley speaking.

Faye, who had tried not to interfere, felt it was time to speak.

'I agree with Mrs Armitage,' she said firmly.

'If you say so, Governor. But how do we know that the girl would like to move?' asked Charles Radley.

'It's easy to find out,' said Faye and nodded to the Chief, who left the room.

A few minutes later she was back with Norah, who was

looking less shy than usual, and even excited, the Chief having explained to her what might happen.

'Come in, Norah,' said Faye. 'We are discussing moving you to another wing. To a cell on your own.'

Norah could hardly believe it. 'To another wing? Oh, please, please.'

'Is there something wrong? Anything you'd like to tell us?' asked Faye.

There was a pause. Norah hesitated. Then she shook her head.

'Very well. We'll have you moved at once, and Norah—'

'Yes, madam.'

'Start buying your painting things again, won't you?'

'Oh yes, madam.' For the first time Norah smiled. 'You bet.'

Still smiling, she left with Mrs Armitage.

'So you and Mrs Armitage were right. She was being terrorized,' said Radley.

Janet Harker gave a wry smile as she rose. 'At least Mrs Armitage didn't say "I told you so",' she said and went back to her office.

'The Chief has a feeling about things. And in her own gruff way she really cares about the inmates,' said Charles Radley.

And Faye added, 'One may disagree with most of her opinions, but it would be unwise to distrust her instincts.'

That afternoon Norah was taken to South Wing. It was much more peaceful up there, for Miss Parrish was a disciplinarian.

She took Norah to her cell. Norah was carrying a small case with her possessions and a roll of drawings under her arm.

'Here you are,' said Miss Parrish, 'on your own.'

'Thank you, madam,' said Norah.

Miss Parrish went into the usual speech which she gave to any new prisoners.

'This is a quiet wing,' she said. 'I won't tolerate noise, bad language or bad behaviour. Obey the rules, keep your person and your cell clean and tidy, we'll get along fine.'

'Yes, madam,' said Norah. 'I'll like that.'

'Like what?'

'Being quiet,' said Norah. She gave a ghost of a smile. Miss Parrish unexpectedly smiled back and Norah thought to herself, 'Why, when she smiles she's beautiful.'

Martha Parrish turned and saw the drawings on the table. She picked up the top one, a painting in primary colours of a farm with a sky of scudding clouds.

'These are rather good. I didn't know you were an artist. Have you trained?'

Norah shook her head.

'It'll look very nice in here when you get these up. Well, I'll leave you to settle in. I expect I'll see you at supper.' She went out, shutting the door behind her.

'I wish I could draw her,' thought Norah. 'Perhaps I could, from memory.' She sat on the single bed and stretched out her arms wide in a gesture of sheer relief. At last, she was free of Lily.

CHAPTER SIX

Faye was in her office. She had just had a call from Martha Parrish to say that Norah had settled in well and seemed more cheerful. Faye wondered if people outside the prison would credit how much time was spent discussing what was best for various inmates; in particular, this time a young and frightened girl. It was never time wasted and, in the case of Norah, they had reached the right decision.

The telephone rang and Penny Halewood's voice said, 'Your son is on the 'phone, Mrs Boswell.'

'Good,' said Faye. 'Put him through.'

A click and Paul's voice.

'Is that you, ma'? Look, we aren't driving down to the boat till tomorrow. Mind if I brought someone to supper this evening?'

'Of course not. I'm afraid I can't get in till eight or later, so it will be a pretty scratch meal.'

'Don't worry,' said Paul, 'we'll fix something for ourselves. See you.' And he rang off.

Faye smiled wryly as she imagined what her kitchen would look like. If Paul so much as cooked his own breakfast it looked as though a tornado had hit the kitchen. She wondered whether to ring Mrs Burton to go round, and decided against it. Let the two boys fend for themselves, as Bill was away.

As she returned to work, she realised that he had not told her the name of his friend. 'Ah well,' she thought, 'it's probably the chinless Chris, if they're going sailing tomorrow.'

A knock at the door interrupted her thoughts.

'Come in.'

It was Janet Harker, looking perplexed.

'I'm sorry to bother you, Mrs Boswell,' she said. 'It's about Peggy Abbott.'

'What's happened?'

'She's had a letter from her uncle.'

'When?'

'Yesterday. An odious letter and it's had a traumatic effect on her.'

'In what way?'

'She's become completely withdrawn again; she's sullen, unapproachable. Refused to report for work this morning, even though she knows she'll be punished for not doing so.'

'But Sister was telling me that she has been doing so well.'

'She has,' Janet said, 'but now she thinks she'll never see her children again. It's not true of course – but now Peggy's lost hope. The Night Duty Officer reported that she was sobbing bitterly for a lot of last night.'

'What does Mrs Armitage think?'

'It's her day off.'

'Just as well,' thought Faye. 'She's not quite fair to Peggy.' But she did not say so. Instead she rang Penny Halewood and asked her to look up the name and address of Peggy's uncle. Meanwhile she went across to the wing with Janet, to see for herself.

She was shocked by what she found. The last time she had seen Peggy was the week before, when she had visited Maternity. The girl had been feeding a difficult child, coaxing it and talking to it. She had looked alive, interested and had smiled at Faye as she passed through. But now, as she lay in her cell, she seemed limp, boneless, like a rag doll carelessly thrown on the bed.

Faye saw her alone, but it was a thoroughly unsatisfactory interview. The girl had indeed lost hope. She only spoke once, and that was when Faye told her that not replying was a form of insubordination and she might have to be punished. She raised her swollen, tear-stained face and said :

'Punish? Already I have worst punishment of all. I never see my babies again. My uncle say so.'

And nothing Faye said could persuade her that it was not for her uncle to decide the children's future.

Giving orders that the girl was to be left in her cell for the day, Faye went back to her office, rang Miss Clarke and had a talk with her. She then asked for the address of Peggy Abbott's uncle.

Penny brought her a filing card, to which was clipped a smaller printed card, which read :

> The Reverend Henry Atanga,
> Minister's Lodging,
> Church of St John and St Jude,
> Leinster Street, W.11.

And below this in smaller lettering :

> The Rev. Atanga is at home every Tuesday and Friday afternoon to see parishioners for counselling and advice.

'How very convenient,' said Faye, 'that today should be Friday. What are my commitments this afternoon?' she asked – and looked at her book before Penny could answer. You'll have to ring Mr Morton and say I must cancel our meeting. Ask him to come on Monday instead. I'll be back by five for my appointment with the Medical Board. And let Mr Radley know that I'm out for three or four hours.'

'What about your lunch, Mrs Boswell?' asked Penny.

'A sandwich in a pub will make a nice change,' said Faye.

'Do you want me to make an appointment with the Reverend?'

'No,' said Faye. 'He'd refuse to see me. But if I just turn up, he'll have to, whether he likes it or not.'

As she drove through the crowded streets on her way to Westbourne Grove, Faye wondered what suggestions would come up at the staff meeting which she was holding next week to discuss the allocation of the money the Home Office was granting. Everyone would have their own particular axe to grind, that was certain. Faye herself was positive in her own mind how she wanted the money spent – in doing away with the wire and the catwalks and filling in the floors. She believed it would make an enormous difference to the atmosphere and amenities of the prison. But she must, of course, observe protocol and let all the rest of her staff produce their own suggestions first.

Her thoughts turned to the object of her drive. She was really worried about Peggy. She remembered the first time she had spoken with her alone, when she had been Governor for only a few weeks. She had at last got the girl to talk, something which neither Janet Harker nor any of the officers had achieved. Most of the inmates were only too ready to talk about themselves but not Peggy. However, it seemed that at last the barriers were down.

Faye, sitting beside her on the bed, had asked her : 'I know that you love your children – why did you leave them alone so often?'

'No food. I had to earn money.'

'The report said the children were underfed.'

'I buy wrong things for the babies to eat. I make them sick. I work and I work – washing up, cleaning jobs, anything, and when I get home the babies are crying, always crying, and dirty. Roosevelt, he get fed up.'

'Roosevelt?'

'My husband. Roosevelt Abbott,' said Peggy, with dignity. 'He say I good girl-friend but lousy wife. He leave his shore job and take another ship.' She paused for a moment. Then : 'When I first know him, he always laughing. We go dancing a lot. That was a good time.'

She laughed suddenly and for a moment Faye saw her as she must have been when she first came to London, vivid, lively and gay. Faye made a mental note to ask Welfare to try and trace Merchant Seamen Abbott. Aloud she said:

'Sister is so pleased with your work, she says you are learning fast. Carry on as you are doing now, Peggy.'

Peggy nodded, 'I will. And maybe I write to my uncle?'

'That would be an excellent idea.'

And later Peggy had written and now she had had her uncle's answer which had flung her back into despair.

The church of St John and St Jude was a hideous red brick monstrosity, built in the 1870's. At the side was an annexe, the Minister's Lodging. Faye was let in by a middle-aged coloured woman (Mrs Atanga? she wondered), who looked at Faye in a somewhat puzzled way, but took her without comment to a small waiting room where a coloured boy of about thirteen and his mother were sitting.

On a table lay a mass of tracts and two Bibles. The boy took a dog-eared pack of cards out of his pocket and started to play with them.

'You better not do that, Norman,' said his mother. 'The Reverend would not like it.'

'Him!' replied Norman with some scorn and went on with his game.

After about ten minutes Mrs Atanga came in and said to Faye.

'My husband will see you now.'

Faye glanced at her companions but Norman was still intent on his game and his mother was dozing.

Mr Atanga's sitting room was not large and seemed also to be his office, for it was plain and functional with a large roll top desk and filing cabinet, two rather shabby armchairs and a text in a wooden frame above the fireplace, 'God is Love'.

All the covers and curtains were a drab monotone. No television. No pictures. A cheerless sort of room, thought Faye, for a lively fifteen year old who had never known any background but her own colourful native village. No wonder that the handsome young merchant seaman had seemed so compelling.

Mr Atanga rose. He was a small, dignified man, with a great sense of his own importance.

'Good afternoon,' he said.

'Good afternoon,' replied Faye. 'I hadn't realised your home was actually part of the church, Mr Atanga.'

'I live and labour in the House of the Lord,' he answered, somewhat mechanically, Faye thought.

He gave a little bow and indicated a chair. 'I do not think we are acquainted.'

'No,' said Faye, 'I'm afraid not.'

'Then you are not a parishioner of mine?'

Again he gave a little inclination of his head, and to her horror Faye found herself doing the same thing.

'I had better come clean,' she thought, 'or at this rate we'll be dancing a gavotte.' Aloud she said 'I must explain to you. I am Mrs Boswell.'

Mr Atanga looked puzzled. 'Mrs Boswell?'

'The Governor of Stone Park prison. I have come to see you about your niece.'

The smile left the clergyman's face. 'Why did you come like this? Why did you not make an appointment?'

'Would you have seen me? You wrote to Miss Clarke that you were too busy to discuss a foolish, wicked girl.'

'That is so.'

'And as it is now really urgent, I had to come this way. I must remind you that I, too, am a very busy woman.'

'That I appreciate. But I still do not know why you think that Peggy is worth all this trouble.'

'Not a sparrow falls, Mr. Atanga. I need not remind you of that.'

For a moment the look of self-importance left his face. Faye realised she must press her advantage. She leant forward and spoke urgently.

'I do not believe that Peggy neglected her children from cruelty or selfishness. She was simply totally unable to provide for them, and too ignorant to go to the proper authorities.'

'She had only to come to me.'

'After you had told her not to show her face again, when she married? How could she? Think of her position. She was very young. She could have coped with her babies at home in her native village with help from the older women, but here – ? She was nearly destitute in a strange country.'

'I told her not to marry him. But she would not listen.'

'She was young and in love. She missed the companionship of her friends at home. Tell me, why did you want her to come over here?'

'To help me with the work of the Lord in this parish. It is a big parish and my wife is not very strong. And –' he added rather bitterly 'I paid Peggy's whole fare myself.'

'So that is part of it,' thought Faye, for it was obvious from his home surroundings that he was not a spending sort of man. It must have hurt his pocket as well as his pride.

'Mr Atanga,' she said, 'surely you as a Minister of the Church can see that Peggy merits compassion?'

'Compassion is for the obedient and contrite, not for the proud and wilful.'

'That is what you said in your letter to Peggy. You also said she would never see her children again.'

'Yes.'

'But that is not within your jurisdiction. It is for the courts to decide.'

'I would go to the courts. Those innocent children should not suffer through a wicked mother.'

Faye was on the verge of losing her temper, but managed to control it. 'Heaven preserve me,' she thought, 'from a sincerely dedicated man. His outlook is so strict and narrow that it is almost impossible to meet him on common ground.' She must try again.

'Mr Atanga, I meet many women in the course of my work. Some of them are wicked. But many of them are unfortunate, and also ignorant. Peggy is one of those. In my opinion she should not be at Stone Park at all.'

Mr. Atanga looked amazed. 'Yet you took her in.'

Faye smiled. 'I am there to administer the prison, not to decide who goes there. She decided to try another approach.

'Mr Atanga – could I talk to your wife?'

He glanced at her sharply. He did not want his wife brought into this. But Faye had a quiet authority which he could not resist. He rose and called his wife, who came in looking, Faye thought, rather cowed.

'This is Mrs Boswell,' her husband told her. 'She has come about Peggy.'

'I hope Peggy is not in trouble again,' said Mrs Atanga nervously.

'On the contrary, she has been doing very well in her nursery training. But I am afraid that now she is deeply upset by your husband's letter.'

Mrs Atanga looked bewildered. 'Letter?'

Her husband spoke quickly. 'Get Mrs Boswell some tea, my dear,' he said, and Mrs Atanga left the room. There was a pause, then :

'I didn't mention the letter from Peggy to my wife.'

'So I see,' said Faye dryly.

'You must understand that I will not let the children see their mother, especially while she is in prison. My wife does not agree with this.'

'I think your wife is right. It is while Peggy is in prison that she needs to see them most. They are all she has.'

'They are my responsibility now.'

Faye leaned forward and spoke gently. 'I cannot believe that a man like you, a religious man, will not let her see her own children. Look at the text over your fireplace – "God is Love".'

There was a pause before the clergyman spoke.

'First she must prove she is worthy of them.'

'I think she's done that. I have seen her at work. But if she has now no hope of seeing them, she will retrogress. I beg you, Mr Atanga, to let your wife bring them to visit. I would not have come here to ask this if I did not know how essential it is for Peggy. If you could have seen her pain and bewilderment when she got your letter.'

For a moment there was silence. Then Mr Atanga spoke. 'It is possible that my letter was somewhat harsh. I am not a cruel man, Mrs Boswell.'

'You don't mean to be,' thought Faye, But aloud she said, 'Then if you would write her a short note, and say she may see the children, you would have done a truly charitable thing, and a wise one too.'

Whilst Mr Atanga wrote his letter to Peggy (it was somewhat stilted and prosy but not unkind), Faye had gone in to see the children, a boy of three and a girl of eleven months. She also had arranged with a greatly relieved Mrs Atanga to bring them to visit their mother.

Then, after the Medical Board and before the rehearsal of a drama group play, which she had promised to attend, she managed to spend a few minutes with Peggy and to give her her uncle's letter. The girl's gratitude and relief were moving and she was vehement in her promise to report for work the next day.

Faye drove home later that evening and she felt that today, to mix her metaphors very thoroughly, at least one sparrow had been saved from the burning.

CHAPTER SEVEN

On the way home, Faye suddenly remembered that Paul had a friend in to supper, and hoped that he would not be in one of those moods when only a violent argument – generally political – would satisfy him. As she put her key in the door, it was opened by Bill. Faye was surprised and delighted, for he had been in Hamburg and she had not expected him back till the next day.

'Darling How lovely!' She hugged him and put her briefcase on the hall table.

Every time she came home she felt the prison receding into the background. It was a welcoming place to come back to. She turned to Bill and gave him another hug.

'Lovely,' she said again. 'I'll go up and change.' For when she went home she always shed her prison clothes, in this case, a plain, dark grey dress. She added, 'I gather from that noise that Paul is in? For the stereo was blaring in the sitting room. Bill nodded.

'Yes. She's a bit of a beauty.'

'She?' Faye laughed. 'I thought it would be the chinless wonder.'

'No, he's calling later. They're going off to the boat.'

Paul's voice from the kitchen,

'Is that you, Mum? You're late.'

'Sorry, Paul.'

'Can we bring supper in?'

'Give me five minutes – no three,' and to Bill she said in a conspiratorial voice 'Ought we to leave them alone? We could go to the Trattoria.'

'No,' said Bill. 'Paul seems keen for us to meet her.'

As she went up the stairs, Faye wondered if Paul was serious over this girl.

When she came down, the stereo was not so loud –

Bill's doing, no doubt – and Paul was finishing laying the table.

'Hullo,' he said and called 'Sally! Come and meet my mother.'

A girl of Paul's age came into the room. She was, as Bill had said, something of a beauty. Thin and dark, with a creamy skin. Her clothes, though casual, had cost money. She carried a bowl of salad which Paul took and put on the table. After greeting Faye in a remarkably poised way, she said,

'I hope supper will be all right.'

'She's quite a cook,' said Paul.

'What about a drink first?' said Bill who wanted one himself.

'Sally doesn't drink, do you, love?' said Paul.

'No,' said Sally. 'It doesn't turn me on.'

Bill offered her a cigarette but she shook her head. 'After supper,' she said.

Paul came in from the kitchen with a dish of taramasalata, a delicious fish pâté which holidays in Greece had made one of the Boswell's favourite dishes. It was followed by Chile Con Carne, and finally an orange soufflé. As Paul had said, Sally was a superb cook. The meal was amicable, without any of the arguments that Faye had anticipated. Paul looked happy and relaxed. Bill had opened some wine which was, Faye noticed, quite wasted on the young pair.

'Where did you learn to cook like that?' Faye asked appreciatively, as Paul demolished the last of the soufflé.

'A Spanish cook we once had taught me.'

'To some effect,' said Bill. 'Our compliments to the chef.'

Paul took the dishes out to the kitchen as the others moved from the dining area to the sitting room. Sally sat on the floor. Faye went into the kitchen to make coffee.

Bill took a cigar, and offered Sally a cigarette.

'Smoke, Sally?'

'Only my own, thanks.' She took a case out of her pocket and lit a cigarette. Bill noticed it was handrolled.

'How much d'you smoke?' he asked. For some reason Sally seemed secretly amused.

'Only two or three a day,' she said.

'That could hardly be called a vice.'

'Hardly.' She inhaled deeply.

Faye came back into the room with the coffee. But Sally refused hers.

'I don't believe in stimulants,' she said.

'You don't drink, you hardly smoke. A model student,' said Bill.

'What *do* you believe in?' Faye asked, genuinely interested. Compared with the girls of the same age that she saw every day, this one seemed so very detached – 'cool' was the way Paul would describe it.

'What do I believe in?' said Sally and drew on her cigarette. Paul came back in and sat in the chair behind her. She leant against his knees. 'I believe in staying loose. Feeling free. Not ever being tied down.'

'I can remember feeling exactly the same thing,' said Faye. Bill smiled at her. Sally looked at them almost as though she pitied them.

'She thinks we're indecently old,' thought Faye. Aloud she said 'What are you reading at university?'

'Social Sciences,' said Sally in a bored way.

'So we're in the same field in a way.'

'Yeah. I had to read one of your books last term.'

Faye was interested. Also a tiny bit flattered. To be a 'set book' was gratifying.

'Was it any help?' she asked.

Sally shrugged.

'Not much,' she said.

Bill spluttered with laughter and Paul smiled.

'I should have warned you about Sally,' he said. 'She says exactly what she thinks.

'So I see,' Faye's voice was rueful. 'What was wrong with it? Too theoretical?'

'Oh the theory was all right. But it doesn't go far enough.'

'In what way?'

'You say the whole concept of prisons should change. Right. But why not abolish prisons altogether?'

'That sounds pretty drastic,' said Bill.

'People only become criminals when they break the law.'

'What Sally means,' said Paul, who had probably heard all this before, 'is that if there were no laws there'd be no criminals.'

'That's idiotic, Paul. Some laws are necessary.'

'Why?' asked Sally.

'To protect society.'

'Society!' There was scorn in Sally's voice.

Paul added: 'And people are often punished for things they didn't do.'

'Not as often as you think. I said in my book that prison should be used far more as a form of rehabilitation than as a punishment. And, of course, many people at present inside, should be having different treatment. But to abolish prisons – that's a Utopian ideal – I'm surprised that an intelligent girl like you should even consider such a thing.'

Faye caught herself up. This was not a girl in front of her at Disciplinary. This was a guest in her house. A guest, moreover, who had just cooked her a delicious dinner. She twinkled at Sally and said,

'Sorry. I was lecturing.'

'That's all right,' said Sally. 'But don't you ever get sickened by your job?'

'Sickened? No. Depressed. Sometimes rather angry. But I'm trying all the time to improve things for the prisoners, which makes it all bearable.'

Sally was not impressed. She shrugged and stubbed out her cigarette in an ashtray.

'You've got a reformer's zeal all right,' she said. Suddenly she appeared bored by the whole subject and changed it.

'I do like your caftan,' she said. 'Don't you Paul?'

'Fine,' said Paul, who never noticed his mother's clothes.

'And I envy you your clothes,' said Faye. 'I wish I could wear them.'

'Why don't you?'

'Can you imagine me turning up at Stone Park in jeans?'

Everyone laughed.

'In your book you say that people should be able to wear what they like in prison.'

'That's something I'm working on,' said Faye. 'I think it's essential. But the prison officers must still wear uniforms.'

'I don't see why. Do your own thing, that's what I say,' said Sally.

'I'm sure –' but Faye stopped. It was no good telling Sally that most of the inmates of Stone Park were there because they had 'done their own thing' regardless of the consequences.

The door bell had rung and Paul had gone out to answer it.

'Come on, Sal,' he called. 'It's Chris. We're late.'

Sally stood up. It seemed, thought Bill, as if she were slightly drunk, but was controlling it, which was odd, as she had hardly touched her wine. She looked at her hosts and grinned.

'It's been fun,' she said. 'You mustn't mind anything I said. I just sound off sometimes.'

'I didn't mind,' said Faye and meant it. 'You must read my other book and let me know what's wrong with Approved Schools.'

'Have you got a coat?' asked Bill.

Faye went out into the hall. Paul was coming down the stairs carrying a small grip.

'Back on Sunday,' he said to his mother.

'Have a lovely sail,' said Faye, 'and take care. Is Sally going with you?'

'No such luck,' said Paul. 'She hates messing about in boats. We'll drop her off on the way.'

A horn blared and raising his voice he called 'Come on, Sal. We're keeping Chris waiting.'

Sally came out of the sitting room with Bill.

'Good-night and thank you, Mrs Boswell.'

'Not at all,' said Faye. 'You must come again.'

She stood at the door as they went out to join the impatient Chris, who moved off as soon as they were settled in the back.

As the car drove away, Paul said to Sally, 'You turned out a sensational meal. Real Carrier stuff.'

'They seemed to like it.'

'What did you think of them?'

Sally answered obliquely. 'The house is nice. And some of the pictures. That Lowry must be worth a bit.'

'That was by way of being an investment. My mother bought it years ago I believe.'

'She must have been attractive once.'

'Most people think she still is.'

'Paul! She must be nearly fifty. I'll give you one thing, she could be pretty terrifying if she wanted. Glad I'm not likely to be up in front of her. He's a bit of a stooge isn't he? Nearly as stuffy as mine.'

Paul tried to be loyal.

'He's a typical businessman I suppose.'

'Oh no, my love. My pa is that. Devoted secretary, carnation in buttonhole, Rolls at the door every morning on the dot of nine. What does yours do?'

'He's not in the tycoon class, like yours. But he does all right. He's a consulting engineer. A bit of an expert. Goes all over the world.'

'I know. Always stays in the same sort of hotels, with the same sort of people. Dreary.' She was suddenly bored with the topic. 'Let's go to a late movie.'

She curled up into the warmth of his arm. Paul was only too willing, but Chris, who didn't go for Sally, said firmly,

'No. We must be up early. Got to catch the morning tide.'

There was silence in the back as Paul and Sally went into a businesslike clinch, which lasted until she was dropped at the flat which she shared with two other girls.

Faye came into the sitting room and started punching up the cushions.

'The kitchen is spotless,' she said. 'What a remarkable girl.'

'Did you like her?' asked Bill.

'She's a wonderful cook.' Faye stifled a yawn. It had been a long day.

'You're evading my question,' said Bill.

'Do I like her? She's amusing. She's got a good mind. But there is something—'

'You bet there is,' thought Bill. And looked at the brownish cigarette stub in the ashtray. A reefer, he was certain. But he would not say anything to Faye, she had enough problems of her own – about three hundred and twenty of them to be exact – and Bill hoped that Sally was nothing permanent in Paul's life. He only prayed that Paul didn't smoke, too, but it was no good worrying too much over the young nowadays. He poured himself a brandy and went to his records.

'Now,' he said, 'what shall it be? The Toccata and Fugue, or some Beethoven?'

He turned to Faye. But the Governor of Stone Park prison was fast asleep on the sofa. Her long day had caught up with her.

CHAPTER EIGHT

Lily Hever was bored and restless. She was also in a very evil temper. Ever since Norah had been transferred to the South Wing, she had been without anyone to order round or terrorise.

There was at the moment no one on the wing who was sufficiently young and frightened to suit Lily's book. There were in fact plenty of young prisoners, 'but nowadays,' reflected Lily bitterly, 'they don't seem to care if they're threatened or not. Don't seem to know what fear means.'

She had tried her stuff on a fragile-looking girl, Valerie, who had just come in. Lily had expected an immediate reaction, but instead Valerie had lifted her angelic head with its long wings of fair hair falling on each side, and had said, in a harsh voice, 'You bugger off, you old bag.' Lily had been shocked. What were girls coming to these days? At her age Lily was confining herself to the merest petty thieving from chain-stores; as for her language, she would not have dreamt of speaking in such a way to her elders and betters.

Lily leant on her mop and lit a fag-end which she had in her pocket. She felt in a nostalgic mood today, thinking of those happy days when she was living a life of luxury, all paid for by other people's money.

For those in authority who increasingly believe that the majority of criminals come from deprived or unhappy homes, Lily was the exception which proved the rule. She was born of respectable and loving parents, her father had owned a small newsagent's shop in Twickenham. She had a happy and indulged childhood and spent her holidays with her doting aunt, a childless widow, who was devoted to her.

When her parents died, Lily was twelve and went to live with her aunt. She was later allowed to go away to boarding school at her own wish. It was there that she learnt her power over other girls.

When she was twenty-six her aunt died, leaving her a comfortable legacy with strict instructions, via her lawyer, to invest it in a business and a house. Instead, Lily proceeded to spend it in a workmanlike manner.

Six years later, she found herself penniless, with a worthless cheque book and a good wardrobe. At the time she was living in a three-star hotel in Bournemouth. She had learnt at school to use an upper-class accent, and she took trouble to behave as the other guests did. She enjoyed a drink before dinner and played a respectable game of bridge and tennis. Being a good-looking woman, she had had admirers among the other visitors, three of whom were serious. Unfortunately, Lily did not like men and could not bear the thought of marriage.

One Saturday she received, through the post, an ultimatum from her bank. No more cheques were to be drawn. Assuming her most charming manner, she borrowed ten pounds from a friendly hotel acquaintance, saying that she had missed the bank and would repay it as soon as it opened on Monday. The following day, Sunday, she borrowed a further fifteen pounds from another friend and repaid the first, with profuse thanks. The next day she borrowed again and repaid the second loan, and so on, until the hotel bill was two weeks in retard and she realised she would have to move on.

She smuggled her luggage out of the hotel and went to Brighton, where she played the same game, which she found stimulating and delightful. She never stayed too long in any one place, and always had at least ten pounds cash in her pocket on loan from a friend. This went on for nearly eighteen months at which time she was staying at Newquay. Ironically enough, she was not arrested for defrauding the hotels, but for stealing a quite worthless brooch at Woolworths for the sheer fun of it. In court, the whole story came out and she received quite a heavy sentence. She was bored to extinction in prison, as well as missing her creature comforts. Her sole recreation was making trouble, until Norah came along.

Now Norah had been removed and all Lily's ingenuity was needed to see the girl again. It was not going to be easy, as they did not go to any of the same classes, nor do the same work, and now that church was no longer compulsory, they did not even meet there.

She noticed Mrs Armitage approaching and quickly whipped her cigarette end out of her mouth, and stuffed it between her fingers, long experience having taught her that this was far less unpleasant than the resulting punishment if she had been caught smoking whilst working.

'Good morning, Chief,' she said, with her most sugary smile. The Chief only nodded and passed on. Lily muttered 'cow' to herself, and made a show of resuming work.

Mrs Armitage stopped to speak to Fran Morris, a big, handsome, raw-boned woman with dark hair. She was in for inflicting 'g.b.h.' on a woman who had tried to take her husband away from her. She was popular with most of the inmates and many of the screws. She was also adored by her husband who visited her whenever possible. She did not much like Lily and showed it. Lily who was, like all bullies, a coward, moved away, wondering if she was being discussed. In fact, Mrs Armitage was asking Fran about Margie Bassett, a girl who had only just come in with a nine month sentence, and who had been in a state of unhappiness bordering on hysteria. Mrs Armitage had arranged for her to share a cell with Fran.

'How is Margie?' she asked.

'Poor kid. She's a bit better. Still in a state. Good thing everyone don't take it so hard.'

'Just as well,' said the Chief.

'It's Joe. Her bloke. They've only been married three months and Margie's crazy for him. No chance of him visiting, Chief?'

'Hardly, as she is in here, and he's in Cricklewood,'

said Mrs Armitage dryly. 'Fran, I'm grateful to you for helping her along.'

The Chief strode off and into Miss Harker's office. Lily watched her go, and then slowly joined the working party who were moving on towards another part of the wing. Somehow, she thought, she must see Norah again. The thought of the girl, probably alone in a cell without anyone to stop her stupid drawing and painting, made Lily furious. Somehow she must see her.

The following day, luck was with Lily. Coming back from the library she saw Norah coming towards her, carrying some books. She looked better, more relaxed with a faint colour in her usually pale face. Lily ducked into a corner until Norah was just about to pass. She put out her hand and grasped Norah's arm. The girl turned with a gasp of fear.

'Lily!' she said. 'You!'

'Yes me, lovey, your old friend. Been missing me, eh?'

Norah didn't answer.

'Or maybe you've been avoiding me, eh? That it?'

Norah shook her head. Lily closed in on her, gripping her arm viciously.

'Oh yes you have. Can't deny it can you? That's not nice is it?' She twisted Norah's arm – lightly. Norah stared at her, shaking a little.

'After all the trouble I took, getting Mrs Boswell to give you a nice little room all on your own. Well, d'you know what you're going to do now? You're going to ask Mrs Boswell if you can come back and share with me, see? Because you miss my company, see?'

'No!' The word was involuntary. At once Lily twisted her arm again, more brutally this time so that Norah gave a little scream.

'So you won't ask her?'

Bravely, Norah shook her head.

'OK then. D'you know what'll happen to you? One day when you aren't expecting it, you'll have a little accident –

to your face perhaps or – maybe your hands. Then you wouldn't be able to do your pretty drawings, eh?'

And she gripped Norah's left hand, twisting the fingers. By now Norah was crying soundlessly, quite terrified. Then, the sound of footsteps. Lily looked quickly round. A prison officer was coming along the landing. Instantly Lily was a loving friend, solicitous, kind, stroking Norah's shoulder and murmuring: 'Poor love – you mustn't cry.'

The prison officer came up to them and Lily was obliged to relinquish her hold on Norah. Instantly the girl ran off, clutching her books, towards the South Wing.

The prison officer was a temporary relief, a Mrs Matthews, and did not know Lily.

'Whats going on?' she asked. 'Who was that?'

'It's Norah Williams from South Wing,' said Lily, sounding concerned and sympathetic. 'She's upset because they split us up, you see.'

'I see.'

'D'you think I ought to go and see her?' Lily's voice was soft and anxious.

Mrs Matthews hesitated for a moment.

'No. You'd better get back to your wing. I'll have a word with Miss Parrish later on.'

'Yes.' Meekly Lily turned away. Inside she was in a raging ferment. She had really scared Norah this time. The whole episode had caused her tremendous excitement. If only that screw didn't say anything to Miss Parrish! But even if she did, Norah wouldn't give her away; she was too frightened.

As it happened, Mrs Matthews did not mention it to Miss Parrish. She had not known the significance of the meeting, and in the worry of her first day, she forgot all about it.

At breakfast the next day, Faye said to Bill, 'Wish me luck.'

'Always, my dear. But why today especially?'

'We are having a meeting to solve the knotty problem of the Home Office grant.'

'I thought you'd made up your mind.'

'I have, but everyone else will have different ideas.'

'If you want my advice . . .' said Bill.

'I do. Very much.'

'Let all the others have a small slice of the cake. Then they won't feel put upon. And you will still have enough for your own major project.'

'That is a sensible suggestion,' said Faye. She did not tell Bill that she had already planned to do this. 'I'll be late tonight. The meeting's at seven. And darling, look up a free evening next week or the week after, and I'll ask Charles Radley to bring his wife to dinner. We must have them soon.'

'D'you want to know now?' said Bill, reaching in his pocket for his diary.

'Tonight will do.'

Paul appeared in the doorway, looking sullen and arrogant and, thought Faye, very handsome.

'I'll be out tonight,' he said, and disappeared as suddenly as he came.

Bill raised his eyebrows. 'What was that in aid of?'

'Sally stood him up last evening. He'd asked her round again and she never turned up. He was telephoning frantically.'

'I'm glad I'm not twenty-one,' said Bill comfortably, and took another cup of coffee.

By a quarter past seven, the inevitable coffee and biscuits disposed of, the meeting in Faye's office was starting to settle down to business. Faye sat at her desk, with most of the staff disposed of round the room. Charles Radley sat on her right, and on her left sat Mr Norton, with his notebook. He had just read out a list of suggestions, which had ranged from building an entire new Welfare Centre, to providing two new prams for the Maternity Wing.

When he had read them all, he added, 'This is a less ambitious suggestion than some of the others, but I myself would like to recommend that a part of the money be spent on bringing our filing system up to date.'

'At least you have a filing system,' said Miss Clarke hotly. 'Mrs. Boswell, can't you possibly consider building a proper Welfare Centre with adequate facilities?'

'If its a matter of rebuilding, can't we enlarge the hospital wing?' The Sister in charge was speaking. She turned to Dr Mayes. 'Don't you agree, Doctor?'

Peter Mayes smiled at her. 'I have had a word with the Governor privately, haven't I Mrs Boswell? I think you will find that she has something planned for us on her list.'

'For most of us, in fact,' added Charles Radley.

'Bless you both,' thought Faye, as the faces round the room looked less hot and angry. Aloud she said, 'Yes indeed. There is, mercifully, enough money for all of us to benefit. Let me see the list, Mr Morton. Please modernise your filing system to the tune of a thousand pounds. Miss Clarke, I can't alas, build a complete new Welfare Centre. But I have spoken to the Works Officer and I think we may be able to utilize parts of the Prison Officers' Block now that so few live in. That would give you three offices and four interview rooms, which would, I imagine, be better than nothing.'

'It would indeed,' said Miss Clarke, who seemed to have recovered her temper.

'Regarding the Hospital Wing, I have talked with Dr Mayes and his staff, and the Works Officer has given us a plan for modernising the bathrooms and lavatories. And I know Dr. Mayes and his staff feel, as I do, that the wing badly needs redecorating in a more cheerful manner, in keeping with today's trend. So I will arrange for this to be done. You and I Sister,' and she smiled at the Hospital Sister, 'must put our heads together with Dr Mayes.' Sister, who had a passion for Dr Mayes, looked pleased at the thought.

Mrs Armitage cleared her throat.

'There is one thing, madam. It's really a request from the prison officers. I said I would pass it on, though I think it's a daft sort of idea myself.'

'What is it Chief?'

'They say the inmates are always grumbling about the food. Not the quality, but the fact that it's never hot. That's why a lot gets left. Personally I think they should eat it and be thankful.' She ended her sentence with an almost audible sniff. Faye paused before answering.

'It is a problem. I quite see your point of view.' (Hypocrite, she thought to herself). 'But on the other hand, it does seem a pity to waste good food. The trouble is that it has to come such a long way from the kitchens.'

'Surely the answer would be insulated containers,' said Radley. 'Like we had in the army,' added Dr Mayes. 'Or on planes,' added Janet Harker. Miss Parrish shot her a glance of dislike. 'Silly girl – showing off,' she thought.

Faye turned to Mr Morton.

'Perhaps you would get us some estimates. We could spend up to a thousand pounds. Thank you, Mrs Armitage for your suggestion, it certainly would be a great improvement.' She glanced at the list on her desk. 'Oh, and Sister Chin-Lin,' the pretty Chinese Sister from Maternity looked at her gravely, 'of course you may have your two new prams for Maternity. Are you sure that is all you need?'

Sister Lin bowed her head and said it was.

For a moment, sensing a pause, everybody talked and murmured among themselves. On the whole a cheerful murmur, Faye thought. Then she picked up her list and gave a little rap on her desk.

'Now that the detailed improvements have been agreed, I want help from all of you regarding the allocation of the bulk of the money. Can any of you suggest one major improvement which would benefit the entire prison?'

She looked round at the faces. For a moment no-one spoke, then Janet Harker said,

'I think the most important aspect is environment. We spend so much time trying to give the women a sense of their own value. How can they develop that feeling in such depressing conditions?'

'Are you suggesting that Stone Park should be run like a holiday camp?' said Miss Parrish scornfully.

'No, I'm not. But I think we should try and improve the inmates' living conditions,' said Janet.

'If you start experimenting with the women, they don't know where they are.'

The two Assistant Governors were glaring at each other. At any moment there would be an open quarrel. Faye said quickly,

'What do you think Mr Radley?'

'I think it would be a good idea to give the whole place a face lift,' answered Charles Radley.

Janet Harker was delighted by this.

'The effect on the women would be tremendous,' she said.

Mrs Armitage sniffed loudly, and Mr Morton said dryly, 'You can redecorate as much as you like, but a prison will still be a prison.'

Faye felt she must give Janet some support.

'I must admit I was thinking along the same lines as Miss Harker,' she said.

Janet looked pleased.

'What conclusions have you reached?' asked the Deputy.

'It seems to me the main problem is overcrowding. The women have to spend far too much time locked in their cells,' said Faye.

'I agree madam,' said Martha Parrish. 'But there is nowhere else to put them.'

'That's when they become so lonely and bitter,' said Janet.

Exactly,' said Faye. 'But imagine the difference if the floors were filled in across each landing? It would remove that depressing impression of being in a cage.'

She saw the Chief and Miss Parrish as they exchanged glances. Both faces showed varying degrees of annoyance.

'Speaking for myself, madam,' said Martha Parrish, 'I would not be pleased if each floor of my wing was filled in.'

'It would double the work of the prison officers,' added Mrs Armitage. 'As things are, I can look up and see at a glance what is happening and where my officers are needed.'

'Always the same cry,' thought Faye and made a conscious effort to continue to look pleasant.

'The answer to that would be to increase the number of Assistant Governors so that each was responsible for a smaller unit,' suggested Radley.

Martha Parrish stiffened. Was this upstart suggesting reducing the size of her own domain? She would not put it past him. Mrs Armitage sniffed louder than ever. Again Faye felt it was time to intervene.

'I think we should remember that we are not here to study our own convenience but to decide what is best for the women in our charge.'

'Exactly,' said Charles Radley. 'Now that we have the chance to do something about the problem of overcrowding, shouldn't we act on it?'

Faye wanted to throw him a grateful glance but restrained herself. Instead she said firmly,

'Filling in these floors would give us the one essential – space. Extra room for classes and association. More televisions. The whole operation would create a far better atmosphere.'

Before anyone else could speak, Mrs Armitage answered quickly, 'I'm sure no-one denies the benefits from the inmate's point of view, madam. But I think we must consider the prison officers as well. It is going to mean twice as much work for them, and we are understaffed as it is.'

Before anyone else could speak, Charles Radley said firmly, 'Perhaps we have gone as far as we can today, Governor.'

Faye, who realised she was sitting on a volcano, answered, 'Yes indeed. Thank you for all your various suggestions. I will see that they are acted on. Regarding the floors, I will think it over very carefully and let you know my decision.'

CHAPTER NINE

Martha Parrish and the Chief went to have a cup of coffee together. They were both urgently in need of a good grumble, for they realised that they were fighting a losing battle over the floors, and each in her heart of hearts knew that the Governor would defeat them.

After half an hour of soothing gossip, Martha Parrish said,

'When are the women going over to wearing their own clothes?'

'Next month I believe. And that's a mistake if ever there was one. It will mean a lot of shopping too. Some of them have nothing fit to wear. What a waste of money!'

They had been joined by a senior prison officer from East Wing who snorted agreement.

'Too true,' said Martha Parrish and rose to go.

'How is the transfer, Norah, getting on?' asked the Chief.

'She's fine. Much more relaxed. She's quite a clever girl with her pencil.' Miss Parrish smiled. 'She did a drawing of me. It's good enough to have it framed. Well, good night Chief. I'm short of officers tomorrow. Three of my prisoners are being transferred and one has to go to Court, which makes us short-handed, so I'll try and get an early night.'

'Yes,' said Mrs Armitage. 'I don't know why they can't give us escort officers who do nothing except ferry the inmates about.'

This was a constant complaint, and one that was fully justified.

As Miss Parrish left, Mrs Roberts the prison officer turned to Mrs Armitage.

'Another cup, Chief?' she said and added, for she was a talkative woman, 'it's strange about that girl Norah

Williams. The library lady, Mrs What's it, the one with the funny glasses, never can remember her name, told me that Norah took all her art books back this evening and didn't take any more out. And she's so keen.'

Before Mrs Armitage could comment on this she added, 'What do you think about this idea of the women wearing their own clothes, Chief?'

Mrs Armitage spent a few minutes telling Mrs Roberts exactly what she did think, and then left. She was going to work late tonight, as her husband had company.

After the meeting the Deputy Governor and the S.M.O. stayed for a short post mortem. The general feeling was that the meeting had passed off better than they expected.

'Old Morton will be blessing you. He's been beefing on about this wretched filing system ever since I've been here,' said Dr Mayes.

'You were a great support, both of you. I'm grateful,' said Faye.

And Charles Radley added, 'I thought at one moment Parrish was going for poor young Janet. What a headline!'

They laughed as the meeting broke up.

'You look very pleased with yourself,' said Bill an hour and a half later. They were having an excellent meal, left ready by Mrs Burton, in front of the fire. Faye was in a dressing gown relaxing. In the background music played softly.

'Everything passed off better than I expected,' said Faye. 'I think it's going to be all right.'

'Filling in those floors sounds like a good idea. I hope you haven't let yourself be talked out of it.'

'No. But I mustn't rush things. By the way, I took your advice about the slice of cake for all of them.'

'Did it work?'

'Yes it did.' She took another mouthful. 'M'm. This casserole is really delicious isn't it? Clever Mrs Burton.'

'All clever Mrs Burton did was to take it out of the deep freeze, thaw and heat it up. You cooked it.'

Faye laughed. 'So I did. I remember now.' She looked at Bill 'You're tired darling. Had a bad day?'

'Frustrating.' He did look tired.

'Tell me.'

'The tests on that new pre-stressed concrete I told you about are disappointing.'

'Won't you be able to use it?'

'Not till they've ironed out the bugs. I'd like to be around for the next few days but that Belgian factory is proving a problem. I must go over tomorrow.'

'What a bore for you. Some problems do hang around.'

'Yours as well as mine eh?' said Bill. 'And of course yours are more important.'

He was suddenly violently irritated by this pretty successful woman to whom he was married. Too successful by half, thought Bill, with some bitterness.

Faye smiled, in what seemed to Bill a complacent way. In fact she was trying to smooth things over.

'You know you wouldn't like it if I wasn't a working woman.'

'I am not likely to have a chance of finding out, am I?' said Bill as he poured himself another glass of wine. He sat gloomily, wishing that for once he could have Faye's full attention. He drummed his fingers to show how irritated he was. Unfortunately, his wife didn't notice. She was far too deep in thought over her own problems.

Mrs Armitage had taken the opportunity of working late. She usually had to leave as early as possible in order to get home to Ted, but tonight his sister was staying the night, so she decided to tidy up the paper work in her office which was in a muddle. It was half past nine when she got up, put on her coat and picked up her handbag.

Outside the lights were turned down for the night. The Admin. corridor was quiet. Mrs Armitage stifled a yawn. 'My, but I'm tired,' she thought. It had been a long day.

She had almost reached the gate when she stopped. Something had been at the back of her mind for the past hour or so – something Mrs Roberts had said about Norah. It was probably nothing but she had a feeling. She turned and rather wearily made her way up the spiral staircase to the South Wing on the third floor. The principal officer on night duty was standing near the top of the stairs. She seemed surprised to see the Chief.

'Did you forget something Chief?'

'No. I wondered if Norah was all right. Number thirty-two.'

'The transfer? Quiet as a mouse. Not a peep out of her. Why?'

'It was only something that Mrs Roberts said. I ought to have come up then. I'm probably fussing. Anyhow let's have a look.'

She walked along the catwalk to the door of Norah's cell and listened. There was indeed not a sound. Mrs Armitage turned up the shutter over Norah's spyhole and looked in.

Norah was lying half off the bed. Her eyes were shut, her face drained of all colour and her wrists were deeply slashed, there was blood everywhere. On the floor lay a broken china saucer.

Mrs Armitage turned to the officer

'Ring the doctor at once. Emergency,' she said urgently. Instantly the Chief switched on the light in Norah's cell, unlocked the door. Moving very quickly she seized a towel which was lying over the washstand and tore it in two. She started to bandage Norah's wrists. The blood was not spurting and it seemed that the girl had missed the main artery. But she was deathly pale and Mrs Armitage could discern practically no pulse. She hoped that the night duty officer would be quick in getting through to the Hospital Wing. She straightened Norah up and put a pillow under her head. After a moment, Norah moaned, so faintly that the Chief could scarcely hear. Then her eyes opened for a moment.

'Thank God,' muttered Mrs Armitage. Aloud, she said in a voice unlike her usual brusque tones, 'Don't worry dearie. You'll be all right. All over now. We're taking you to hospital.'

Norah's eyes were shut. Mrs Armitage heard voices in the distance. The stretcher at last. They'd taken their time. Looking at her bloodstained hands she rose to rinse them in Norah's basin. As she did so she noticed the pictures on the walls. They had all been scored across, defaced by a thick black pen, destroyed, ruined.

Norah opened her eyes again, finding it difficult to focus. She felt very faint and ill. But she realised dimly what was happening. She wasn't going to escape after all. They would take her to hospital, they would make her well and then send her back to share with Lily. With a superhuman effort of will, like the final spurt of a hunted animal, Norah flung herself off the bed and out on to the catwalk, avoiding the Chief's outstretched arms as she tried to stop her.

'No,' she cried. 'Not any more,' and flung herself over the rail and into the wire net, two floors below. She screamed as she did so, a high thin scream which echoed round the high-ceilinged wing. There was a jangling crash as her body hit the wire mesh, far below.

In the Boswell's sitting room, the atmosphere was peaceful. Bill's irritation had passed and Faye had temporarily forgotten her problems. Indeed, they were both more than half asleep, when suddenly, brutally the red telephone, the direct line to the prison, rang.

For a moment Faye was dazed. Then, quickly, she answered it. It was Peter Mayes. She listened while he spoke and then said,

'I'll come along at once.'

She rang off. Bill noticed she looked very pale.

'It's Norah,' she said. 'The girl I told you about.'

'The girl who you thought might be terrorised?'

'Yes. She's attempted suicide. I must dress and go in.'

'I'll drive you,' said Bill firmly.

Faye didn't argue. She was thankful to have him.

Only once on the way to Stone Park did she speak. She suddenly struck her hands together and cried in an anguished voice, 'That bloody net! It must go!'

It was very quiet in the hospital wing. Norah was in a small cubicle, heavily sedated, a nurse sitting by her side. Both her wrists were now professionally bandaged and she was attached to a drip.

Mrs Armitage, her face grave, was waiting in the passage for Faye. Faye put out her hand and touched her arm, but did not speak. Dr Ward, one of the junior medical staff, came up to them. He was a bumptious young man, who Faye did not greatly care for.

'How is she, doctor?' she asked.

'Her face may be scarred for life,' answered the young doctor briskly in what Faye thought was a rather heartless way. 'But she'll live all right. We've sent for Dr Mayes. He always says to contact him in any emergency, and I suppose this is one.'

'I imagine so,' answered Faye dryly. She was glad to hear Peter Mayes' voice in the passage.

'Sorry I couldn't get here sooner,' he said. He looked down at Norah, then turned to Faye.

'Could you wait outside?' he said.

'Of course. We'll go to the Centre.'

She turned to Mrs Armitage, whose eyes were scored by deep lines beneath them. She did not look her usual vigorous self. Faye took her by the elbow and the two women turned away towards the Centre where they sat and talked in subdued voices.

'What happened?' Faye asked

Mrs Armitage told her story. Faye noticed that her hands were shaking a little and she clasped them together as she spoke.

'How horrible,' said Faye. 'But if it hadn't been for

you she would have been dead by the morning. You've probably avoided a tragedy. I'm grateful to you.'

'I wonder if I have. She doesn't look too good to me,' said Mrs Armitage and added, 'It should never have happened. She spoke a few words before they put her out. Not very coherent, but it seems that Lily caught up with her. She thought you were going to make them share again.'

'Me? But I . . .'

'I know, madam.' The Chief's voice was suddenly a whiplash. 'But you know our Lily. I wish I could make her pay for this. That poor girl. I'll watch Lily like a lynx after this.'

They paused as they came into the Centre and stood looking up at the shadowed gloom of the nets above them. It was no longer quiet up on the Wing. Stifled sobs came from some of the cells, shouts came from others. Prison officers were going from cell to cell, soothing, calming, scolding. A woman's voice cried 'For Christ sakes put the bloody light on' and a moment later a light went on, and another.

'I'd better go up,' said the Chief.

'I'll wait for Dr Mayes,' Faye said; and she sat, hoping that the women would not be too upset by this. So many of them were already in a disturbed emotional state, and something like this could plunge them into hysteria.

Peter Mayes joined her. He reported that Norah was in a state of deep shock. 'She's broken a couple of ribs, I think,' he said, 'but it could be more serious. She might have damaged her spleen too. I'm sending her to hospital. The ambulance is on the way.' And he added, 'It's a hell of a way to fall – poor kid.'

Yes, thought Faye, she had looked like a child, a very tired child; and then blamed herself, thinking bitterly that, if she had had the courage of her convictions, she would have been on the way to getting rid of the wire by now. She thanked Dr Mayes, and went up to join Mrs Armitage, who met her at the top of the spiral stairs.

'It's quietening down a bit now,' the Chief said.

'I supose there was an uproar when it happened?'

'She screamed as she fell.' The Chief's voice spoke volumes.

Faye tightened her hands on the rail and looked down. 'One thing is certain. These floors must be filled in, and the wire must go. This had made up my mind for me.'

And ruefully Mrs Armitage said, 'I hate to admit it, madam, but I'm afraid you may be right.'

Mrs Armitage stood in the hall of her flat. Ted and his sister were still up. She could hear the telly. She glanced at her watch. Only a quarter to eleven. It seemed like the small hours. The Governor had insisted on giving her a lift home. It was not out of their way, she had said, and her husband was driving. And indeed the Chief had been thankful: for once in her life her legs seemed to have given way

She would give herself a cup of tea before going in. She did not feel up to chatting with Ted and Flo yet. Stupid to be shocked. Just another of 'them'. But that girl Norah – it was silly – but there was something about her. Could it possibly be innocence?

Mrs Armitage knew she was talking rubbish to herself. She took out the brandy she kept for emergencies and poured out a tot, reacting against the taste which revolted her.

She sat at the kitchen table relishing the strong tea; soon her nerves were in less of a jangle. Funny how she had had a moment of sympathy and agreement with Madam. Heaven knows they did not agree normally.

She was a lucky woman, that one, Mrs Armitage thought, with her looks and her brains and her husband. With his handsome face and white hair he looked for all the world like the 'older man' in the advertisements Attentive too. 'Sure you're all right?' she had heard him murmur to Madam. Anyone would be all right, with a husband like that to go home to. And plenty of money all round. I don't suppose she's ever had any worries in her life, she thought. And that coat!

For Faye, in her hurry, instead of putting on the sensible coat she invariably wore to work, had snatched up a mink coat, which Bill's Canadian associates had given her after a particularly successful job he had done. It was a thing she would never have bought herself, but for all that it was a possession she greatly prized.

Mrs Armitage gave a sniff and poured another cup of tea. She was rapidly returning to normal. In a minute she would go in and chat with Ted and Flo. But first she had better let Parrish know. After all, it was her wing; and it was quite likely that the orderly officer would have forgotten to ring her.

She went into the hall and dialled a number.

'Martha?' she said.

Martha Parrish was watering her many house plants, which she tended meticulously, when the telephone rang. With a 'tch' of annoyance she went to answer it in her carefully kept room. She had several good pieces left her by her parents from the Georgian Rectory in Suffolk where she had been born and brought up. She and Jack had loved antique and Victorian furniture and had picked up some bargains in the fifties when they were setting up house. All of her furniture was beautifully polished. The room was bare of ornaments and had a faintly masculine air about it. There were few books for Miss Parrish was not a reader, and no record player since she did not care for music. There was, of course, the inevitable television, she had few friends and would have been lonely without the vicarious company the various programmes offered.

Martha Parrish was one of nature's misfits. She would have been a handsome man. Even as a child, before the days of universal jeans, her feminine clothes sat unkindly on her. She had a man's energy, and lack of sentimentality. An aunt had sent her away to a boarding school and there she had fallen in love with a girl, Jacqueline, whom she called Jack. Jack was a little older than herself. They were a handsome pair and had been completely happy together. Theirs was a very real relationship. Long before they left school they had arranged to live and work together. They decided to be teachers. Jack, 'the brainy one', had taken a teachers training course and a good degree. Martha had gained high honours in Domestic Science. After graduating, they had spent a year going round Europe in a small car. On their return, they had little difficulty in getting a post at a large girl's boarding school in the West Country.

For seven years they were completely happy together, living in a small cottage. They had a garden and two handsome cats. They had joined the sailing club and often won races. They were popular at the school and would probably have stayed until retiring age, if Jack had not gone sailing one squally day in early May. Martha had had to drive a class of senior students to a practical exam in the nearest big town. When she returned they told her the news.

Jack had capsized – in itself nothing. She had gone over the side and was preparing to right the dingy, when a well-meaning but ignorant party of holiday-makers in a large hired launch had tried to come to her rescue. Ignoring her frantic cries of, 'Keep away!' they had closed on her: their boat had swung round and Jack had been struck on the head by its screw. She had died instantly.

The Commodore of the sailing club, who had told Martha the news, was reminded of the expression 'a woman turned to stone'. From that moment she seldom laughed or smiled. For the rest of the term she struggled on at the school, but she was too unhappy to continue. Always a disciplinarian, she was now very strict. Taking advice from an old friend of her father's whom she liked and trusted, she decided to try for the Prison Service. She was used to working with a concourse of girls and her ability to keep order was an asset. After a spell at an open prison as domestic science teacher, she applied for the post of Assistant Governor at Stone Park. She had now been there for seven years. She was remote from most of the staff, her only friend being the Chief, and even they never met outside the prison. She was a very lonely woman, who had developed her brisk abrupt manner as a defence during the terrible months after Jack's death.

During the past year she had developed a kind of relationship with one of the long-term prisoners. But it was in every sense unsatisfactory, since meetings were almost impossible. Martha's one hope was that eventually they would set up home together: and even as she thought this she felt disloyal to Jack. Her constant dread was that the woman would be transferred. No-one at Stone Park knew any of this, of course.

When she heard the Chief's news over the telephone, she felt deep regret. Norah had roused in her an emotion she had never felt before, even for Jack. She felt maternal towards the girl. During the past week or two Norah had become less withdrawn. She looked at the drawing that Norah had made of her. It was strictly against the rules to take presents from the inmates, but Martha had argued to herself that as she had given Norah the drawing block, it was in fact her own property. One of the cats came in through the cat door and jumped on to her knee. She stroked it absentmindedly. She prayed that Norah would be all right. Norah, oddly enough had not found her frightening as most people did, but had seen the beauty behind her closed in face and abrupt ways.

'I must go and visit her,' she thought, 'as soon as it is allowed.'

After dropping Mrs Armitage at her flat, Bill drove home with some speed; he had a flight booked at ten the next morning, and he wanted to put in an hour in his office first. As he put the car away, Faye packed his case. She felt it was the least she could do after spoiling his evening. He dropped asleep almost at once, but Faye could not sleep. She made herself coffee and went into the sitting room. She opend her briefcase and took out some work, always for her a sure panacea.

She remembered what a judge had said to her once when she asked him if he could sleep after condemning someone to a long sentence. 'I never take my work home with me, my dear. I would have no peace if I did. When I leave court, I leave the whole case behind me.' All very well for him, he was not responsible for the people who came up before him. Whereas, try as she could, Faye could not rid herself of the feeling that she could have prevented this evening's near-tragedy. She had mistrusted Lily Hever from the beginning, but because Norah had been so quiet and gave no trouble, she had not looked into the case carefully enough. She had accepted the fact that Norah was completely withdrawn. It was a common enough condition in prison, but in Norah's case it had led to disaster. When the girl was well enough, the psychiatrist must see her. Come to that, perhaps they should see Lily Hever too. Faye forced herself to study some of the figures the works officer had given her, and to stop worrying.

It was past three o'clock before she went upstairs and fell into an unrefreshing and uneasy sleep. When she woke Bill had already gone. She left early for Stone Park, and rang the hospital to which Norah had been taken. When the Sister heard who it was, she was put through to Mr Downes the surgeon in charge of the case. He was not entirely happy over Norah. She was going into X-ray later that morning. They would keep Faye informed.

There was a knock at the door and Charles Radley came in.

'Sorry to hear about last night,' he said. 'Horrid for you.'

'Worse for Norah,' said Faye.

'I suppose so,' Charles Radley was unable to share the Governor's deep personal involvement with the inmates.

'Even the Chief was upset,' Faye added. 'We gave her a lift home. Bill said her hand was trembling when he helped her out of the car.'

'I don't believe it.'

'It's true. She even agreed with me about the floors.' Faye leant forward, speaking urgently.

'Nothing will stop me doing this now. You do see that, don't you?'

'There is just one thing, Governor. In view of the long term plans for the prison, do you think this expense is really justified?'

As he spoke, he nodded to the wall, where an architect's drawing was pinned up – the drawing of a long, mainly low, red brick building, resembling a large motel, with only the visitors and their cars missing.

This was the new Stone Park, designed to be finished in ten years. Whenever she was more than usually depressed, Faye used to look at the drawing, as a pilgrim looks towards Mecca. But in answer to Radley's question, she shook her head firmly.

'It's a wonderful plan,' she said, 'and I hope I shall be here to see it completed. But we can't endure the present conditions for another ten years. In a way it's worse for the staff than the inmates.'

'The staff don't all think so,' said Radley.

'Oh, the Old Guard. I know. But you should hear the younger ones on the subject of the net. No, my mind is quite made up. I am going to the Home Office tomorrow.'

Charles Radley nodded, with resignation. What an obstinate woman this was. But all he said was:

'Then we must have a meeting with Morton and Henry Mackie.' Mackie was the Works Officer.

'How soon do you think we can start?' asked Faye.

'Once the plans are ready, not too long. We'd better warn Cricklewood that a really large working party will be needed. Shall I see to all that for you?'

'Thank you. It would be a great help. One other thing,' Faye said. 'As you know, I've decided to get rid of the uniforms, and I can see no point in delaying it. They can go into their own clothes next month. I'll arrange the drill for the changeover with the Assistant Governors; and they can tell the inmates.'

Radley smiled. 'They know already – most of them anyway. The grapevine has been working overtime.'

'I should have guessed,' said Faye.

Later that day Faye went to the hospital to see Norah. But the girl was asleep, under sedation. The X-rays had shown that Peter Mayes had been right. She had indeed broken two ribs and her spleen was damaged. They were going to operate.

Some days after this, Peter Mayes was in the saloon bar of the Golden Lion, a pub near Stone Park. He was in a bad temper as Janet Harker had stood him up for a young doctor with a yellow Maserati. This was the second time it had happened, and he was beginning to think he must change either his car or his bachelor habits.

A registrar from the local hospital came across.

'Mind if I join you?' he said. 'I'm Rodney Stone, Downes' registrar.' Mr Downes was the surgeon who had operated on Norah.

'Hi! Sit down,' said Mayes. 'What's your tipple?' After he had ordered, he said, 'Norah didn't look too good today.'

'Norah?'

'The splenectomy I sent in.'

'No. I'm afraid not. She's deteriorating. She was in bad shape when she came in. She'd lost a lot of blood. Sister says she has absolutely no will to live.'

'I'm not really surprised. Poor little creature.' For a moment Peter Mayes considered Norah but she was no longer his patient, and this was his free evening. A wasted one, thanks to Janet.

The doors opened and a comely girl with red-brown hair and an exceptionally good figure came in. She waved to Rodney Stone and joined another girl at a table.

'Who's that?'

'Vanessa Campbell. One of our new physiotherapists. Bit of a dish.'

'M'm. Go and ask her over – and bring the other girl too.'

From force of habit Rodney obeyed the older man. After all he was the Senior M.O. at the prison. He did so unwillingly, for he had designs on Vanessa himself. But luck was against him. Half an hour later Peter Mayes came out of the pub with the girl. They drove away together, both of them anticipating an amusing evening.

In the hospital, Norah was dying. She lay, hardly conscious; but her mind, though clouded, was still functioning. She was thinking in a hazy way about her mother, and the stream at the bottom of the garden.

Norah had been a happy, mischievous little girl. Her mother had spoiled her as she was an only child. They had lived in a cottage in a small town in Essex. When Norah was nearly three, her parents had taken her, one Bank Holiday, for a coach trip to the seaside. There was an accident and her mother was killed. From that moment, Norah's chance of happiness was gone. She was sent to live with her grandmother, a woman who neither liked nor understood children. She became a sulky, bewildered child.

Later, when her father married again, she rejoined the family circle. Her noisy stepbrother and sister had no use for her at all. Her stepmother began ill-treating her. When she was six, a neighbour complained to the authorities and Norah, a 'battered baby', was taken into care. She was fostered by various families, none of whom wanted her. When she was nine, her father died and she went to an orphanage run by his union. She was kindly treated, and discovered her talent for drawing, which was not discouraged. But she made no friends either among the staff or the other children. With her slow, almost retarded ways, she was difficult to communicate with.

Through all her vicissitudes she had thought of her mother, her mum, as a talisman who made life bearable. In bed at night she would talk silently to her.

When she reached Stone Park, and found that she could buy drawing and painting materials, and that she was sharing with old Mrs Weekes, who was garrulous but kind, life began to have some meaning again, though she was still painfully shy. Then Lily Hever had singled her out as a likely victim, and her existence became intolerable again.

She stirred and open her eyes. It was getting dark, she thought, she could hardly see. But someone was sitting near her, someone was holding her hand in a warm, firm grasp. Into her failing sight came a face, a beautiful face that she remembered.

'It's all right Norah. I'm with you.'

A great relief came over Norah. Mum was here at last. After all these years it had come right.

'Don't go,' she said. It was the faintest of whispers, barely audible.

'No, darling. Never.'

Happy for the first time for years, with her hand confidently in her mother's, Norah lapsed still deeper into unconsciousness.

The minutes and hours ticked on, the night noises of the ward outside the drawn curtains, seemed far away, and Martha Parrish sat, growing stiff and tired, and wishing she was a religious woman and could pray.

At half hourly intervals a nurse came in, took Norah's pulse and left again. As the first false dawn showed in the sky, night sister came in.

After a moment, she said,

'You needen't wait any longer Miss Parrish. She's gone,' and added, 'Poor girl. But she looks happy doesn't she?' For Norah, who had never laughed in her life, had a smile on her lips.

CHAPTER TEN

Faye announced her decision about the rebuilding the following month. It had been accepted calmly by the staff, on the surface at any rate. The Works Officer was preparing the plans for the Home Office approval and Charles Radley was in touch with Cricklewood about the actual work.

All the day-to-day maintenance work was usually done by men who were in Cricklewood. The women enjoyed having the odd male about. Naturally they tried to use them as messengers to the outside world and for cadging cigarettes. Even, usually unsuccessfully, for some quick sex. But during the rebuilding it would be a matter of twenty or thirty men being permanently on the wings and the staff – even Janet Harker – were prepared for trouble.

More immediately, Faye was putting into operation her plans for the women to wear their own clothes. On the appointed day great hampers were sent up to the Wings, together with the women's suitcases which they had handed in when they were admitted. They were all sent off to change, and then gave their suitcases back. They then filed past the open skips throwing their prison clothes in bundles into one and their shoes into the other. The atmosphere was light-hearted. On Janet Harker's Wing, as they filed past the hampers someone started singing (to the tune of 'Nuts in May'), 'Here we come throwing our gear away' and it was taken up right through their wardrobes, ending of course with 'knickers' which caused the inevitable giggles which the word seems to rouse. On Parrish's Wing, 'the quiet wing', the atmosphere was much more subdued, but there was, even there, a feeling of release.

Faye went up to the Wings in the afternoon of the

changeover, during Recreation. She was astounded at the difference it made, to see the women in their own clothes. The deadly monotony of the uniforms had gone. Some of the clothes were garish, some shabby. But they were now a concourse of women with their own personalities. A lot of giggling was going on among the younger ones, 'Like it madam?' Faye was asked several times.

Mrs Armitage walked about with her mouth buttoned up, but Janet Harker was very approving of the whole operation.

'Have you seen Peggy Abbott?' she asked Faye.

'No.'

'It's amazing. Of course she's been a different girl since the children have visited, but this –' she called into the room where Peggy was watching television.

The girl came out towards them. She wore a bright scarlet cotton frock with a full petticoat and red stockings on her long thin legs. She smiled at Faye flashing miraculously white teeth at her. Faye remembered the woebegon figure crouched on her bench the day she had taken up her duties.

'Well, Peggy,' she said. 'Not much longer now.'

'Only eight weeks, lady.'

Fran interrupted. She looked bigger and more blousy than ever in black trousers and a lacy shirt.

'Ever seen Peggy dance, madam?' she said. She turned to the record player and put on a record. And Peggy danced, her whole body moving in time to the music. Some of the other women joined in and others stood clapping. Even Margie, usually so depressed, joined in too.

Faye smiled and went to Janet Harker's office. Mrs Armitage saw her coming and moved away. She had avoided the Governor except for duties ever since the evening when Norah had attempted suicide. She didn't quite know why.

Janet Harker was watching the women, smiling.

'The Chief is a prophet of doom,' she said. 'She thinks

we'll have trouble tonight, they are all so over-excited.'

'Let's hope she's wrong,' said Faye. She added, 'Where's Lily Hever?'

'In her cell. She won't come out. She wants to stick to her prison clothes. Says her own are too good for this stinking hole.'

'Are the other women talking to her?'

'No. They all realise that she was the cause of the Norah business. None of them will even give her the time of day.'

'One can't blame them. I must try and do something about the wretched woman.'

And Faye went back to her office where Mr Morton was waiting for her with his usual file as well as plans and estimates for the filling in of the floors. The paper-work seemed enormous but, she told herself, she had only herself to blame.

There was a knock on the door and Charles Radley came in. Faye thought he had of late looked worried and rather worn. She feared it was something to do with his home life.

She had asked him to come to supper with his wife one evening and he had said he would consult Beth. Later he had accepted without a great deal of enthusiasm. Faye had the feeling that it was Beth Radley who was unwilling to go and wished she had not asked them now. What a pity it was, she thought, he was such a nice man.

'Am I interrupting, Governor?' he said.

'No,' said Faye. Mr Morton has just finished.'

'One of the women on remand has asked to see you.'

'Can't you deal with it? You usually cope with the remand people.'

'She's a new reception. She especially asked to see you.'

'Why?'

'She wouldn't say. It's a drugs case. Name of Benedict.'

The name meant nothing to Faye.

'Very well,' she said. 'Bring her along in an hour or so. Mr Morton and I should be through by then.'

At the door Charles Radley's good-looking but rather gloomy face brightened.

'I had to go up to North Wing. I found myself in the middle of a fashion parade.'

Faye laughed and Mr Morton permitted himself a prim smile.

'I know. They're loving it. Mrs Armitage is prophesying utter disaster.'

'She's probably right at that. She often is.'

The door shut on him and Mr Morton and Faye went back to their work and managed to finish it. Faye even had time to have a much needed cup of coffee before Charles Radley came back. He was alone. He had left the remand prisoner outside with the prison officer who had brought her down. He was carrying a card with details of the prisoner's reception.

'The Benedict girl is outside, Governor,' he said.

'What's she in for?'

He laid the card on her desk. Faye read 'Benedict, Sarah, age 20. Flat 1, 3 Lauriston Road, St Johns Wood. Charged at Beech Street Magistrates Court with possession of two ounces of cannabis. Remanded in custody for seven days. No previous convictions.' She looked up. 'Then why wasn't she given bail?'

'She was offered it, and refused.'

'How odd. Where was she picked up?'

'At a café near Russell Square.'

'Well,' said Faye, 'we'd better have her in.'

Radley went to the door and said something to the two people outside. Faye looked at the card again. 'Lauriston Road, St Johns Wood.' For some unexplained reason the address rang a bell in her mind. She could not imagine why.

'Sarah Benedict, Governor,' said Radley's voice.

Faye looked up. In front of her stood Sally, Paul's Sally. She looked defiant and was wearing a small triumphant smile. For a moment Faye was completely shocked.

'Sally!' she said involuntarily.

Charles Radley and the prison officer both reacted to this. It was the last thing they had expected. With an effort Faye pulled herself together. Outwardly, she was the prison Governor, calm and authoritively. Inwardly, her heart was beating faster than usual. This was the girl whom she thought her son loved, whom he might want to marry.

She spoke very calmly. 'Why did you want to see me, Sally?' she asked.

'It's about my bail, Faye,' said Sarah.

Charles Radley stiffened and the prison officer looked as if she had been struck.

'Madam!' they said simultaneously.

'Sorry. I always call you Faye to Paul. It slipped out – madam.'

Faye was beginning to get angry. The girl had done that deliberately.

'Answer my question,' she said.

'It's about my father. When he hears about this he'll ring you, or something, and say he'll stand surety for me. Well, you can tell him I don't want him to.'

'Why not?'

Sally's smile was by now rather insolent.

'That's my business isn't it?'

'I suppose so. What was your bail set at?'

'Fifty pounds. Not much. But I didn't want bail at all.'

'As you wish.'

There was a moment's pause. Sally was beginning to feel somewhat scared. It was hard to equate this stern, rather hard woman with the comfortable person in a caftan who had praised her cooking the first time they met. Sally had always thought she might be different on the job. For a fleeting moment she wondered whether to change her mind about bail. Then her native obstinacy decided her to go through with it. Faye was speaking again.

'I shall have to tell the Home Office that I know you

outside the prison, to declare my interest, and to hand you over to Mr Radley the Deputy Governor. He will look after you. In any case he usually deals with the remand wing. Goodnight.'

'Goodnight, madam,' said Sally with one of her secret smiles. The prison officer glanced at Charles Radley, who nodded.

'Come along,' said the officer brusquely and took her out.

'Don't go, Charles,' said Faye. And realised she had used his Christian name.

'Sorry,' she said. 'I always call you Charles to Bill.'

'That's fine, Faye,' said the Deputy Governor and they both smiled. He shut the door and came across the room.

'A pity Officer Barnes heard all that,' he said. 'It will be all over the prison tomorrow. It must have been quite a shock to you.'

'It was,' said Faye. 'She's my son's girl friend. I had not the faintest idea.'

The Governor had disappeared and the worried mother was predominant.

'I wonder if Paul knows,' she said. 'This may be a terrible shock to him.'

'I wonder,' thought Radley. 'He may be on drugs himself.' Aloud he said 'Why don't you let me take you to have a drink? You could do with one I expect.'

Faye shook her head. 'I must get back,' she said. 'Fortunately I've finished here. I'd like to be there when Paul comes in.'

Privately Radley thought that his Governor was being rather naive. He could not believe that a university student would be so astounded at the idea of a girl-friend smoking reefers. Aloud he only said, 'Has he been going out with her for long?'

'He may have been. He's seen a lot of her lately. He brought her home about six weeks ago. She cooked supper for us. She's a superb cook. Afterwards she told me what was wrong with my books and how to run this place. She knew it all.'

'They do, don't they,' said Radley wryly.

'Then, one evening, Bill and I had been to the theatre together. He'd parked the car in that car park behind the Saville Theatre and we were walking towards it along one of those rather sinister Soho streets when we ran into Paul and Sally, as they came out of a café. We gave them a lift home –' Faye stopped and said, 'Of course! That's where I heard her address. Anyhow, after we got home, Bill went up to bed and Paul and I had a long talk, most unusual nowadays. I realised, even if he didn't, that he is in love with her.'

'And she with him?'

'It's hard to say. She's very cool.'

'Do you like her?'

'I don't know. I think she's bright enough and quite talented. She certainly did her best to put me in my place. She's violently anti-establishment, of course.'

'Naturally. Does she live at home?'

'No. Lately she's taken to sharing with two other girls, one of them a schoolfriend. From what Paul told me, her father does sound rather pompous and hard to live with.'

'Big business?'

'Yes. Property I believe.'

'Is there a mother?'

'No.'

'I see. Well, I'll have a go tomorrow and see what I can find out. If only the silly girl had let herself be remanded on bail.'

As he reached the door, Faye shot a question at him.

'Charles, what do you think about pot?'

'Smoking it is an offence.'

'You know that's not what I meant. I've heard people I respect say that this law should be changed, that it's no more habit-forming and far less of a health hazard than drinking.'

Radley's face stiffened. He is a bit rigid, thought Faye,

maybe it's a good thing in here. I'm apt to be too liberal over the woman, perhaps.

'You'd better ask Peter Mayes about that,' Radley was saying. 'He's involved with the Drug Unit here. My own feelings are that smoking pot is potentially a very dangerous pastime.' Then, realising that he had not been supremely tactful, talking to the mother of a possible addict, he made his exit and Faye packed up for the day and hurried home.

CHAPTER ELEVEN

She need not have done so. Paul was not in, and there was a message, via Mrs Burton, that Bill's flight had been delayed and he would not be back till later.

'Splendid,' thought Faye, 'I shall be able to do all the dreary domestic things that need doing. The records are in an appalling mess. Paul never puts them away. I can ring Laura too, (Laura was her elder sister) she loves a long natter, and I never seem to have time. And I'll go through my clothes.'

In the event she did none of these things. She did, in fact, ring Laura who was delighted and embarked on a long and boring story about her newest grandchild, when Faye suddenly thought that Paul might be trying to ring her and made an excuse and rang off, thereby causing sisterly offence. She switched on the television and caught the tail end of a news item of a plane crash in Northern France. With Bill spending a quarter of his life flying, she had long ago conditioned herself not even to consider the possibility of a crash. But tonight she was in a kind of panic and even went so far as to ring flight enquiries, only to be told by a superior voice that as Flight BE359 hadn't yet left Paris, it was unlikely to have arrived at Heathrow. It was a wretched evening. She kept thinking of Sally locked in her depressing cell. No need to feel sorry for her, she was there at her own wish. But, in a way, Sally was part of Faye's family life, rather than her official one, and the thought of one of the family being behind those bars, subject to the inevitable prison discipline, was worrying indeed. That night, she saw the prison through the eyes of an inmate, and did not like all she saw.

The evening seemed endless. If only Paul would ring! – but why should he? He hadn't the habit of ringing and besides he probably didn't know about Sally if she'd been arrested unexpectedly. Faye realised that her thoughts were fluttering like a trapped bird. She must pull herself together. After a bath and the merest pretext of a meal, she turned as usual to work, neglecting the domestic chores she had planned, and absorbed herself in a turgid directive to 'All Prison Governors in Great Britain and Northern Ireland' which had lately arrived from the Home Office and which took much concentration to read.

In her cell, Sally was looking in some dismay at a long typed sheet which Officer Barnes had given her.

'NOTES FOR YOUR GUIDANCE TO THE ROUTINE ON THE REMAND CENTRE

On admission you will be allocated to a room which you will occupy until you return to Court, or are transferred. You are responsible for keeping it clean; failure to clean it when asked to do so is a reportable offence.

7.30 am Rising bell.

7.45 am You will be unlocked for breakfast; you must be up and dressed when the officer comes to your room. If you have an application for the Governor, you must go at once to see the Principal Officer. (See Note below on 'Applications').

8.00 am You collect your breakfast. The medicine bell is rung. Return to room.

8.15 am If you have booked for the MO, you will be taken to him.

8.30 am You will be unlocked. Leave your room tidy: the bed must be made. Your room will be inspected.

9.00 am EXERCISE – weather permitting; this is for 1 hour and is compulsory. You will only be excused on the instruction of the Doctor.

10.00 am To workrooms.

10.30 am All new admissions and women for discharge will see the Assistant Governor and Chaplain. Legal aid forms will be given to those who need them.

11.30 am Return from work. Medicine bell is rung. Collect dinner; go to room.

1.30 pm Unlocked and taken to work.

3.30 pm Return to wing for tea. Medicine bell is rung. Go to room.

7.45 pm Supper served. Medicine.

APPLICATIONS There are two lists on the piano: one for the Governor; and one for letters, doctor, welfare, education officer, chaplain, etc. These lists are collected at 4.45 pm each evening. Late admissions should see the Evening Duty Officer to have their names added to the lists.

Applications for Governor must be made for:

Clothing . . . you may have clean clothes sent in when you have been given Governor's permission. If you do not have permission, the clothes will not be received at the gate.

Spending of Private Cash for Remands and Trials . . . To spend private cash on Tuesdays and Fridays, you must book on Monday and Thursday evening to see the Governor. Should you be brought on the wing too late to book, you must ask the Evening Duty Officer to add your name to the list ... or report to the Principal Officer at 7.45 am on Tuesday/Friday. It is too late to ask to spend at 10.30 am.

Welfare Officers . . . Book on the appropriate list. If you have family problems, they will endeavour to help you.

Medicine . . . If the doctor has prescribed for you, a

bell is rung three times per day; it is your responsibility to go to C3/19 when you hear the bell.

Letters and Visits . . . Read the information lists on the wing.

Canteen . . . All women on Thursday; except Remands who choose not to work.

Bells . . . These are to be rung in emergency only – if you persist in ringing for trivial requests, it is possible someone who really needs assistance will be missed.

Sally read it in horror. And this, she thought, is for people on remand! People not yet even proved guilty. What would it be once one was sentenced? So this was Faye's liberal modern prison, she thought scornfully. In this Sally was being grossly unfair to the authorities in general and to the Governor in particular. The amount of reforms and improvements that have been made in the past thirty years are remarkable; and Faye was working all the time towards a freer atmosphere.

Sally stretched herself out on her bed (there was nowhere to sit except a hard chair) and wondered how long a sentence she would get. She wondered, with a grin, what Paul would think of it all.

Paul was sitting with some friends in a small club in Camden Town. They had seen the news item tucked away in the corner of a page of the evening paper 'Property Tycoon's daughter on drugs charge.'

'Did you know, Paul?' asked Judy, a great friend of Sally's, much addicted to pot herself. She was a pretty girl spoilt by a very bad skin. She had the sleepy eyes of a habitual smoker.

'Mm,' said Paul, who hadn't, but who was giving nothing away.

'Wonder how long she'll get?' said Andrew, a masculine-looking boy with shoulder length hair and thick black eyebrows.

'May not get any time. It says here that she was "in possession of", not "pushing".'

Judy ordered some more coffee.

'Smoke, Paul?' she asked and passed him a cigarette.

'Thanks,' said Paul and took it. But he did not in fact smoke it.

For half an hour they discussed Sally. She was popular despite her rich and despised father. They arranged among themselves to visit her.

'If it's allowed,' said someone.

'It'll be allowed all right. She'll get preferential treatment, with Paul's mum in charge.'

'Don't you believe it,' said Paul. 'She's right on the book, my mother is.'

When Bill finally got home late, in rather a bad temper, after a difficult day and an uncomfortable flight, he was not best pleased to be greeted by Faye who was obviously not her usual calm self. Fortunately she had had the sense to make him some supper and to pour him a stiff drink. It was not until he had drunk the one and eaten the other that she embarked on the saga of Sally Benedict.

'Benedict,' said Bill. 'So that's who she is. You know who her father must be? It's an unusual name.'

'No. Who?'

'The property man, of course. Rolling. And quite a ruthless sort of fellow I gather. Besides being a terrible show-off. Always in the gossip columns.'

'That may well explain Sally,' said Faye thoughtfully.

'Anyhow,' said Bill. 'Tell me what's happened. And give me another drink first.'

Faye told him. When she had finished Bill said thoughtfully, 'I thought she might be on reefers that evening. She was smoking handrolled cigarettes.'

'Surely we'd have smelt it? That horrible sweet smell.'

'Not if she'd only used a little, just enough to make her a bit high. And I was smoking a cigar. Remember how her mood changed?'

'Yes,' said Faye. 'Why didn't I realise it? But why did she take the risk?'

'She probably gets a kick out of doing something illegal,' said Bill. 'How was she when you saw her?'

'She seemed in a strange way pleased with herself.'

'She wasn't selling the stuff?' asked Bill.

'No. If she had been she wouldn't have been offered bail. It's Paul I'm worried about.'

'You think he's keen on her?'

'That too. But what I meant was, is he involved in this reefer business?' Faye tried to put the question very calmly.

'We've got to face it, he may be.'

At that moment the front door slammed. Paul came in. He looked very much on the defensive.

'Hullo,' he said laconically.

'Hullo, darling. Have you eaten?'

'No. I'll get something.'

'I'll get it for you. Cold chicken and salad do?'

'Fine.'

Faye went into the kitchen, thinking hopefully that he might talk more easily to Bill. In this she was wrong. When she went back with his supper, both men were sitting in silence. Bill was reading the *Evening Standard* and Paul a rather crumpled copy of the *News* which he had brought in. For a moment she felt irritated with Bill. Surely he could understand the dichotomy she was in over Sally? Then, she remembered that Bill had always avoided any sort of heart-to-heart talk with Paul, ever since he was five years old.

Tonight, she would leave the ball in Paul's court. She went across and put on a record, rather softly. After eating his supper, far too quickly, Paul got up.

'He's not going to say a word,' thought Faye.

She was wrong. At the door Paul paused.

'So you've got a new visitor,' he said to Faye, defiantly.

'Yes,' said Faye, deliberately brisk. 'I saw her. Did you know about it?'

'No. I was going out with her last night, but she didn't show. When I rang the other girls they said she hadn't turned up. I thought she might be out with her ghastly father. Then she wasn't at any lectures today and later one of the others saw the paper.'

Bill grunted and lit one of his cigars.

'Rotten for you, Paul,' he said in a gruff way.

'Worse for Sally,' answered Paul.

'No, Paul,' said his mother. 'It's deliberate on her part. She could have had bail but she refused it.'

'She can't want to stay in jail?' Paul was amazed.

'You explain it, darling. I can't.'

'Anyhow,' said Paul, 'I'm going to visit her. You can't stop me.'

'Of course I can't,' Faye answered smoothly. 'It's Sally's decision. She can have daily visitors and she can name them.' And she added, deliberately, 'Has Sally got a cat?'

Both men stared at her.

'What on earth has that to do with it?' asked Bill.

'Nothing,' said Faye. 'Except that remand prisoners can have up to three visitors a day. And one of my predecessors had to determine whether or not a cat constituted a visitor.'

She had achieved her object. Bill gave a splutter of laughter and even Paul looked less strained. Then Bill spoilt it all by asking,

'Did you know she was on reefers Paul?'

Paul looked at him angrily.

'Oh what the hell?' he said. And slammed the door and left the room.

Bill looked at Faye ruefully.

'Sorry,' he said.

Faye was for some reason feeling less tense.

'Don't be sorry,' she said. 'It was a question that had to be asked and I think that now we know what the answer is.'

The following day, Charles Radley saw Sally in his

office. She sat facing his desk. Near the door sat a prison officer. Radley was trying, without much success, to find out what made Sally tick.

'I'm not a pusher,' Sally was saying. 'But if I've got some, anybody can have it.'

'Don't you see anything wrong in that?'

'What's wrong with a little pot? It's harmless.'

'I think I must warn you that if you talk like that when you go for your hearing, the Magistrate won't like it.'

Sally looked defiant. 'I have to say what I believe. They can bully me as much as they like. It's all so stupid.'

'All I'm doing is giving you advice for your own good.'

Sally looked scornful. 'I'm not going to pretend that I've seen the light.'

Radley was getting irritated. What a maddening and pigheaded girl this was. He tried again.

'What I'm saying is, that you can mess up your own life if you want. Is it fair to give cannabis to someone who's never used it before?'

Sally shrugged. 'It's just like buying someone a drink. A joint is just the same. Makes you feel better and it's not dangerous.'

'You're wrong there. The majority of addicts start on so-called soft drugs.'

'So what?' Sally was enjoying the argument. 'I don't see any difference. A lot of older people drink too much, but nothing's done. But if we younger ones want a smoke it's wrong. Tell me why?'

Damn the girl, she was challenging him. His slight north country accent became more pronounced.

'Because,' he said sensibly, 'so often, when people smoke cannabis they get reckless and think they can handle anything. Then, before they know where they are they're in trouble, or on to the hard stuff. Tell me, have you ever met anyone who's a real addict?'

'Of course I have,' Sally was indignant. 'Lots of us smoke at university.'

'I was talking about the hard stuff – heroin.'

'Oh!' She was nonplussed for the moment. 'Yes, of coursc I have.'

Radley realised she was lying. She was like a child, he thought, despite her age. But an obstinate and dangerous child. He only hoped that the psychiatrist whom she was seeing that afternoon would have more luck with her.

The next day, with the reports in his case, he went to see the Governor. He hoped for her sake that the affair between her son and Sally Benedict wasn't serious. He wouldn't care to have that one in the home. In the Centre he ran into Miss Parrish as he stopped to check the hospital book on the table. She had seemed even more curt than usual lately and he wondered why. He made an effort to pass the time of day.

'Well, Miss Parrish,' he said, 'getting ready for the great move?' For it had been arranged that, during the rebuilding, the inhabitants of one Wing should double up with the other.

'Thank you, Mr Radley. I can handle my own problems.'

She spoke very stiffly. Radley knew that she resented his appointment. 'Well, it's not my fault that the woman is a lesbian,' he thought. For alas, poor Martha's carefully kept secret was known to the entire prison staff and to the authorities as well. It was, in fact, the main reason for her not having been promoted.

Radley closed the hospital book with a bang.

'Sad about Norah Williams,' he said, having seen her name in the book.

A sudden twinge of pain crossed Martha's usually impassive face.

'Yes,' she said shortly. 'Very sad.' And added with a touch of malice. 'How are you coping with the Governor's friend?'

'Who's that?' asked Radley, knowing perfectly well.

'The drug addict.'

'Oh she's no addict. She's not hooked on anything,

except herself. Trouble is, she can run rings round me in an argument.'

He was deliberately knocking himself, trying to get on a better footing with Parrish. But she would not respond.

'No doubt you'll charm her in time, Mr Radley,' she said curtly, and moved away.

Radley went up the stairs to Faye's room. So that was it! She had had an affection for the little waif, Norah. That was why Norah had blossomed during her weeks on the South Wing.

Faye was sitting at her desk. She was looking, as she had since Sally's appearance, strained and somewhat weary. Not surprising, thought Radley. She must be wondering whether Paul is going to be in trouble as well and, if so, how it will affect her. When he had said as much to Peter Mayes the night before, the doctor had given one of his ironic smiles.

'She'd be in good company,' he said. 'Have you noticed lately how many distinguished folk have had drug trouble with their young?' Not that that would be any consolation to Faye. Today, however, she was smiling.

'Look at this,' she said. 'You remember that I told you about Peggy Abbott's uncle?'

'The Old Testament priest?'

'Yes. He's sent me an amazingly generous offer. He's found a flat for Peggy near his church, and he's going to pay for the furnishing of it, but Peggy can choose. It will make the whole difference to that girl to have somewhere of her own, instead of squalid furnished rooms.' She put the letter in her 'In' tray. 'I must write and thank him – warmly. Now, what can I do for you?'

Dammit, thought Radley, now I'm going to worry her again.

Aloud he said, 'Psycho's report on Sarah Benedict.' As he expected, the smile left Faye's face making her look tired and tense and five years older.

'Is it all right?' she asked anxiously.

'Yes. They've only had a preliminary talk, but he says

that she seems balanced and fully responsible for her actions. It's all here in his own jargon.' He laid the report on Faye's desk. I'd say myself—' he paused.

'Go on, I want to know.'

'I'd say she was just one of those poor little rich girls who think they can do what they like, that the law doesn't apply to them.'

'I think it's more than that. I think her father may have something to do with it.'

'You mean she's trying to draw attention to herself?' asked Radley.

'Something of the kind. I know she's got a social conscience of a sort and is probably deeply ashamed of his wealth, and the way he earned it.'

'I gather she's been brought up regardless. She seems to resent it.'

Faye looked at him. 'I think she's created a role for herself as an outcast and a rebel. She's acting it out now.'

Radley's tone was ironic. 'If she isn't careful she'll act herself into getting six months or a year, when she goes back for trial in a few days time.'

'I know.' Faye remembered how much longer he had been in the prison service than she had and put a question to him. 'If this was a man's prison, what would you do?'

'I think I'd try a bit of shock treatment as a last resort.'

'What sort of shock treatment?'

Radley told her.

She thought for a moment and then said, 'This is a last resort isn't it?'

'Thank you. I'll do my level best. A term of imprisonment would do that particular girl no good at all.'

He left the room and from the Centre he rang Dr Mayes.

'Peter,' he said. 'Can I come and see you? I need your help.'

CHAPTER TWELVE

The next day, Mrs Armitage was in the Admin. Corridor as Faye came out of her office. As Faye came downstairs, she stepped forward.

'There you are, madam. I've just heard something which I think you ought to know.' She seemed almost embarrassed.

'What is it?' asked Faye.

'Your son, madam. He's got a visiting order to see the Benedict girl.'

'When?'

'This afternoon.'

Faye was shaken by this. Not by the fact that Paul was visiting Sally. But rather by his not having mentioned it. She had seen him this morning and he had not said a word.

To Mrs Armitage she merely said in her most level voice. 'He is a friend of hers, Chief. If she wants him to visit her, I can't interfere. Thanks for letting me know.'

Mrs Armitage gave one of her rare smiles. If only she smiled more often, thought Faye. Then the Chief said:

'It's a good idea of yours about the clothes madam. They all seem much happier.'

Faye restrained an impulse to shout 'Hooray'. She merely smiled and went on her way.

Paul and Sally were sitting in the visiting room, at a bare wooden table. At another table sat a remand prisoner, a coloured woman, who was being visited by two friends. At intervals they gave little bursts of laughter, which Paul found irritating. What on earth was there to laugh at in this dreary place?

The prison officer, as a rule, never listened to the prisoners' talk, it was either too poignant or too boring, but today she found it difficult not to look as though she were listening avidly. 'After all,' she thought, 'this is madam's son, and a good-looking boy he is too, though why he comes visiting in those jeans, I don't know. Still, these youngsters are all the same nowadays, no matter who they are.'

'At least you're not in those awful prison clothes,' Paul was saying to Sally.

'They've gone, didn't you know? Your mother's got rid of them. It's only just happened. Some of the screws don't approve. I'm glad. I wasn't looking forward to prison knickers.'

Paul found it hard to be as flip as she was.

'You don't look too pale,' he said.

'I've only been here for a few days, stupid.'

'Is there anything I can bring you?'

'Yes, some books. I've posted you a list today. You needn't bother to come yourself, come to think of it. Faye can have them sent along.'

Paul was taken aback at her insolence.

'You're dead wrong. She wouldn't do that.'

'Why not?'

'Wouldn't it show favouritism? Not fair to the others.'

'God, Paul, you are square.'

There was a pause. Then,

'What about your father?' asked Paul.

'What about him?'

'Have you heard from him?'

'Not a word. I expect he's furious that I wouldn't accept his surety for bail.' She chuckled. 'That's why I did it.'

Paul found it increasingly difficult to talk, knowing that that wretched screw had her ears wide open. Not for the first time, he wondered how his mother could stand working in this dreadful place. To Sally he said. 'I wish you'd told me.'

'Told you what?'

'That you were going to do this. Refuse bail.'

'How could I tell you? I didn't know they were going to arrest me. I was waiting for you when it happened.'

'I know.'

'Pity you were late. If you hadn't been, they might have nicked you too.'

Paul spoke without thinking. 'No they wouldn't. Because I hadn't—'

He stopped. He knew it would infuriate Sally if he said he hadn't a smoke on him. But she guessed what he was going to say, and reacted to it. Her beautiful face was twisted with anger.

'You are a prig, Paul. Sometimes I wonder why I bother with you.'

'Sometimes I wonder too.' Paul was beginning to lose his temper. 'You don't give a thought for other people. Has it crossed your mind that this is a pretty hellish situation for my mother?'

'Too bad,' though Sally didn't sound remotely regretful.

'She wants to help you, you know.'

'She does not,' Sally very definitely. 'She won't see me or even talk to me.'

'But she can't. It's regulations. She knows you at home so she can't.'

'You do know it all don't you? You're just part of the Establishment, with Mummy sitting upstairs in the Governor's office.'

To his astonishment Paul heard himself saying,

'What's so wrong with that? Somebody's got to do this dreary job and if you ask me she's doing it well. She told me herself that everything takes a hundred years at Stone Park and she's got the uniform rule changed in only a few months.'

'Sure,' said Sally. 'It's no good asking me to be fair. Firstly, I disapprove of prisons. Secondly, I'm in one.'

'You needn't be,' said Paul.

Not till I'm sentenced. But after that – you wait till I tell the Magistrate what I think of the law about pot. He'll dish me out a hefty sentence.'

Sally sounded pleased at the thought. Paul could not

understand her at all, and said as much. For a while they argued, fairly amicably, in the old way, and then Paul said,

'When shall I come and see you again?'

'It's hardly worth it, is it? I'll be sentenced on Friday, and after that I'm not allowed nearly so many visitors.'

Paul could have hit her for her idiocy! He also wanted to touch her; it was unbearable sitting here without even being able to hold her hand. How did people bear it, he wondered. No wonder that tensions in here were so great.

The officer spoke.

'Only ten minutes more,' she said to no-one in particular.

Paul said what he had meant to say earlier. He spoke softly,

'Sal – shall I ring up your father at home and ask him to visit you tomorrow?'

Sally shook her head.

'That's the last thing I want. I love Daddy, but Christ how I despise everything he stands for.'

Then she said, 'When I come back here, I don't think you'd better visit, Paul.'

'Why not?'

'It's not much fun sitting just looking at each other like this. Besides, we don't agree about much do we? And I'd hate to get you into trouble.'

For a moment Paul thought savagely of breaking the regulations and taking her in his arms. She was right, it was an impossible situation.

He rose. 'All right, Sal. I'll see you get those books.' He added, idiotically, 'Take care,' and left.

When Sally got back to her cell she found that her single bed had been moved out and bunk beds moved in. She turned to ask the officer what had happened, when the Deputy Governor appeared on the scene.

'Hullo, Sally. Sorry about this,' he indicated the bunks. 'We try to give people on remand a room of their own, but we're short of space this week. So I'm afraid you'll have to share with Linda.'

Miss Flaxton had arrived with a young woman, about the same age as Sally, shabbily dressed in a frayed caftan. She was thin and pale, her light brown hair looked lank and unwashed. She had a paper carrier in her hand.

'Come in Linda. This is Sally. I think you'll find you have a lot in common,' he said blandly and left. Miss Flaxton tipped the contents of the carrier bag on to the top bunk and took it out with her. The two girls looked at each other. Sally was intrigued, but Linda seemed quite incurious and detached. She moved to the one chair and sat down. Sally sat on the lower bunk.

'Hi!' she said.

Linda looked at her. She seemed to have some difficulty in focussing. Sally realised that she was evidently not very particular over what is now called 'personal hygiene'. 'What a pong,' she thought.

Linda spoke in an educated voice.

'What's your name?' she said.

'Sally.'

'What are you in for?'

Sally could not stop a touch of bravado coming into her voice.

'Drugs,' she said.

Linda, who hadn't been interested, suddenly came to life. Her head whipped round.

'You holding?' she asked.

Sally was puzzled. 'Holding?' she said.

'Did you bring any in?' asked Linda eagerly.

Sally shook her head. Linda slumped back in the chair.

'What . . . what are you in for?' asked Sally. For some reason she was scared of this girl.

'Same as you. What are you on?'

Sally hesitated. She suddenly felt very young and inexperienced.

'Grass,' she said, and added, 'It was good stuff, the best. From Morocco. Cost me a packet.'

Linda smiled sourly.

'Christ!' she said. 'The fuzz'll be nicking people for sucking lollipops next.'

On his way back to his office, Charles Radley looked in on the Governor.

'She's moved in,' he said.

'Good.'

'By the way, both the wings seem to be quite calm since the women changed into their own clothes.'

'I know. I'm thankful. The Chief was anticipating ructions.'

'She was wrong and you were right,' said Radley.

'Evidently. I'm going home early tonight,' Faye said. 'Will you stay around for a bit? I hope your scheme with Sally works.'

'So do I,' thought Radley as he went into his office. That Benedict girl was quite unpredictable. Supposing this plan of his worked in reverse and she too became addicted to hard drugs? That would be too bad, he thought, grimly, and rang up his wife.

Beth Radley had a splitting headache. It had been a miserable day. Her class of infants had been especially difficult and she had had what was virtually a reprimand from the Assistant Head. She was seriously considering giving up teaching. She could work in a factory instead, longer hours, but much less exhausting. Charles wouldn't approve, of course. He had this strong feeling for public service. Beth was beginning to feel she did not give a damn for public good. She just wanted to be happy again. But it didn't seem likely: Charles was only interested in those wretched women he worked with. The very thought of the prison made her feel sick. Her mother kept urging her to have a baby, but it didn't seem to happen. Just as well. Her work made her feel she wasn't much good with children. In any case, it was weeks since he had made love to her; he either came home exhausted and went straight to sleep after his meal, or else, after boring her with some prison problem, he would leave her to watch the television and take a mass of work he had brought home into his room and work till the small hours.

The telephone rang. She guessed what it was before she answered.

'All right,' she said and knew how disagreeable she sounded. 'No I won't expect you till I see you – if then.'

She slammed down the receiver and, to her horror, burst into a torrent of tears.

When Faye arrived home that evening Bill was already in. He realised that she was in something of a state about Paul, and for a while he let her talk on. If he ever grew somewhat bored with the goings-on at Stone Park, he used to tell himself that being a Governor was a lonely job, and that he was the only person with whom Faye could let her hair down.

He himself was worried over Paul, too, but he felt that the boy would not make a complete fool of himself. If only that little piece Sally had not been quite so attractive physically. It must be hell for Paul. He must collect his thoughts and listen to what Faye was saying. She was telling him of Paul's visit to Sally.

'It must have been awful for him, Bill. Can you imagine what it's like to see someone you love brought in by an officer? To have everything you say overheard? Not to be allowed to touch? It's better than it used to be. At least people can stay for two hours now.'

'Why,' asked Bill 'was it once shorter?'

'Until quite lately. Only one hour. Even after travelling all day to get there. Inmates have told me that it takes at least half an hour to unwind, to be able to talk.'

'I can imagine,' said Bill. 'Still I think it was extraordinary of Paul to go and see her.'

'He's in love with her, Bill.'

'All the same he might have considered you.'

'When you were twenty-one and in love would you have thought of your mother first?'

'Probably not. But in these circumstances it was a damn fool thing to do.'

'I don't agree with you,' said Faye. 'In the circumstances he would have been a moral coward if he hadn't visited her.'

Bill did not agree, but he did not say so. Instead, he turned the conversation by asking how her first major reform was working.

'The clothes, you mean? It's a great success.'

'No objections from the staff?'

'Some of them don't like it – but, for a miracle – Mrs Armitage approves. She told me so today.'

'You'll win her round yet,' said Bill.

Faye smiled. 'I rather doubt it.' She looked at the time. 'It doesn't look as though Paul is coming in. Shall we eat?'

In the cell, supper had come up. Sally was sitting on her bunk, eating off her tray. On Linda's tray was the same meal, untouched. Linda sat with her head in her hands.

'Why don't you eat?' asked Sally. 'It's not too bad.'

Linda shook her head. 'No appetite,' she said.

They sat for a while in silence. From outside came the clatter of knives and forks and the noise of voices. Then Sally noticed the wedding ring on Linda's finger.

'You married?' she asked.

'Not any more,' said Linda bitterly.

'No family?'

'No. Christ! You're a one for asking questions, aren't you?'

Sally found herself apologising. A great deal of her cool had left her since Linda had come to share her cell.

'Sorry,' she said. 'I was interested. You see, I've never known anyone who took hard drugs before.'

She sounded as though she was paying Linda a compliment. The elder girl realised this.

'Perhaps you'd like my life history?' she asked ironically.

'Not if you don't want to tell me.'

Linda laughed shortly. 'I'll tell you, baby. In one sense it started in a "desirable country residence" in the Hampshire gin-and-tonic belt. In another, it started one summer in Oxford, at my first Commem., when a sweet little hophead undergraduate gave me a pill. Just for the fun of it. Then I started to smoke a little like you do; just to see the colours more brightly and hear the music more clearly. You know?'

Sally nodded. She was enthralled, though she wished Linda didn't smell so bad. The other girl was still talking. 'And then, and then, and then . . .' she broke off suddenly, she was shivering. When she spoke again it was almost a cry for help.

'You haven't got . . . ? No. Of course not. God, I feel awful.'

Sally was horrified. This was not at all how she had imagined things.

'Can't they do anything for you here?'

Linda shook her head. 'I told them I was off it.'

'Why?'

'Because if not, they shove you in a ward with a lot of screaming old junkies, which is sheer bloody hell. Or they shoot you some stuff that takes away the pain but doesn't stop the shakes in the morning.'

She had clasped her arms round herself and sat swaying backwards and forwards, in obvious distress.

'Sure you haven't any—?'

'No!' Sally almost shouted it. 'You know I haven't.'

Linda was suddenly vicious. 'You wouldn't have, would you? Your kind never do. Just in it for kicks aren't you? You haven't any idea – oh God.'

She rose shaking.

'Here,' she said. 'Help me up top, baby.'

Sally rose and helped her on to the top bunk. Then, her appetite gone, she took away both trays. She came back and lay, her hands behind her head, on the lower bunk. She wouldn't admit it to herself yet but she was beginning to regret this whole episode. She had meant to show her father how much she despised him. Instead, she was seeing a side of life which she had thought would be romantic, but which was in reality squalid and terrifying.

By the time Paul came home, it was late and Faye was already in bed in her bedroom. She heard voices downstairs and Bill's was raised. After a few minutes Paul came into her room. She had expected him to be in an argumentative, or angry, mood, instead he came in and sat on the end of her bed looking somewhat rueful. With a shock she realised that he was a little drunk, a most unusual state for him, who drank practically nothing.

'I've been out with Chris,' he said. 'Father is furious with me for going to see Sally. He can't understand.'

'I can,' said Faye, feeling as she said it that she was being disloyal to Bill, but it was Paul who was most important at this moment.

'How was Sally?' she asked.

'She seemed all right. In some odd way she's enjoying being inside. How can she?'

'She can enjoy defying us all. And she may be hoping to get some reaction from her father.'

'She's unlucky to date. She says she's going to blow her top off to the magistrate when she goes to court again.'

'I was afraid of that. Perhaps something may happen to make her change her mind.'

'What could happen, now?'

Faye wisely kept her own counsel. After a moment Paul lit a cigarette.

'Mum?' he said.

'Yes?'

'Sally said you and father would be going through hell wondering if I was on pot. She sounded rather pleased about it. Anyhow, are you?'

'Going through hell? No,' said Faye untruthfully. 'But we did wonder.'

'Would you mind?'

'Be your age, Paul.'

'Yes.' Paul blew out a smoke ring. 'Well I'm not. I don't mind if other people are, don't think I disapprove or any of that lark: lots of my friends are. But I loathe the smell and it doesn't send me. So you and father can stop worrying.'

'Thank you for telling me darling.' Faye hoped she did not sound as relieved as she felt. Paul was sitting on the edge of one of her feet and she was beginning to get pins and needles in it. But she didn't want to break this rare moment of confidence. After a moment he spoke again.

'About Sally and me . . . She said there wasn't much point in meeting any more. Trouble is I don't think I'm basically a political animal and she very definitely is.'

'Do you mind very much?'

'Of course. Like hell I do. She's a marvellous girl in some ways. But after today I don't see much future for us,' and he added in an airy way, 'Thought you'd like to know.'

'Thank you darling.' She realised he was nearly asleep. 'What about bed, now?'

'Right. See you in the morning.'

He pecked at the air above the top of her head, and walked rather unsteadily from the room. Faye felt an overwhelming relief. Now, she thought, even if Charles Radley's scheme doesn't work, at least Paul will be all right. And realised how selfish a mother could be.

Later she went to his room. He was sound asleep, his clothes scattered about the floor. He looked about twelve years old. She tidied his clothes and went back to her own room.

Bill was ready for bed when Faye returned to her room. He wanted to hear what Paul had said to her, and was deeply relieved at what she had to tell him. He had been worried by what Paul had told him about visiting.

'It sounds de-humanising,' he said. 'Can't you do anything about it?'

Faye told him what some of the men's prisons were doing, playing music through a loud speaker to relieve some of the tension, having a tea bar where visitors could buy tea and snacks, and the like.

'We'll probably try that too,' she said. But Bill felt it wasn't enough. He was right, it was a difficult problem. The inmates longed for visitors, but the tension of visiting was so great that the visits sometimes did more harm than good.

Later, Bill was snoring gently, but it was some time before Faye fell asleep, to dream that she was a prisoner being visited by Mrs Armitage, whilst Paul stood by in prison uniform.

The next morning Paul did not put in an appearance. It was some days before he was communicative, but this was no less than Faye had expected.

When she reached her office, later than usual, she found a note on her desk. A short letter. 'It worked. Charles Radley.' She rang through to him at once and he came round to see her.

Sally had woken suddenly. It was quite dark and the prison lights were out. She had been dreaming of having a picnic with her father, of all people. A very happy dream. Outside a clock struck one o'clock. She woke slowly, reluctantly, then realised what had woken her. From the top bunk came the sound of a low shuddering moaning, punctuated by an occasional sob. She looked up. Linda's arm was hanging down from the edge of the top bunk. It was trembling violently, in the dim light.

'Linda,' whispered Sally.

There was no answer. The moans continued, an almost animal sound.

Sally was in a panic. She longed to stay where she was, and not to get involved, but realised this was impossible. She got up quickly and stood on her bunk. Linda was lying on her back. Her whole body was shuddering in a rigor. Her mouth was open, her eyes rolled up with the whites showing. Her breathing was very bad and she was panting violently.

Sally touched her hand. Linda's whole body arched violently. She did not seem human at all. Sally rushed to the door which was, of course, locked. She rang the cell bell, repeatedly, at the same time beating on the door with her hands, and calling,

'Help! Somebody, please, help!'

'How is the girl Linda?' asked Faye when Radley had told her this.

'She was taken at once to the hospital wing and given a shot,' answered Radley. 'Mayes is looking after her. He doesn't give her long, says she's a pretty hopeless case.'

'Poor creature . . . and Sally?' asked Faye.

'She wouldn't go back to sleep until she heard Linda was all right. And then she refused a sedative.'

'Good for her. It can't have been much fun, seeing what full withdrawal symptoms were like. I hope we did the right thing.'

'I think we did. Sally has asked to see me. I'm going up as soon as I've finished Disciplinary.'

'Let me know what happens. Is it tomorrow that she goes to court?'

'Yes,' said Radley. 'I thought I'd look in if you could spare me for an hour or so.'

'Yes. Please do, Charles. I shall be holding my thumbs.'

The next afternoon Faye was in the Centre checking

the 'Letters Withheld' book, when she saw Charles Radley coming down the Admin. Corridor. He was smiling.

'We appear to have lost a customer,' he said.

'Sally?' said

'Yes. The magistrate – it was old Carter-Brown – gave her a great haranguing and she listened quietly. Then gave her an opportunity to speak and she spoke, rather well, I thought. Said she knew what hard drugs could do in terms of suffering and human life, and how soft drugs could lead on to the others.'

'And old Carter-Brown?'

'He was pleased at the effect he thought he'd had on her. He said he'd been meaning to give her a stiff sentence but in view of her change of heart, etcetera, he'd only fine her and put her on probation.'

'Thank goodness,' said Faye.

'And believe it or not, her father was in court. He took her out. To his Rolls I presume,' added Radley dryly.

So that, thought Faye thankfully, was that. She went on to South Wing, for Sally was only one of many, and the day's work must go on.

CHAPTER THIRTEEN

At last the work was in progress. North Wing was finished, and in place of the wire and the catwalks there was, on each of three storeys, a wide open space with the cells opening on to it, divided at one end into extra rooms for classes or activities. The greater part was mainly recreational, and the women had far more space to circulate, nor did they have to spend so many hours locked into their cells. The decorative scheme for each wing was different and Faye had been glad to see the end of the yellowish-cream brickwork.

At the moment North Wing was giving hospitality to South Wing where the work was going on. As the two Assistant Governors were violently opposed to each other's ideas, a certain amount of tension was building up between them.

One morning, a few days after South Wing had been evacuated, Lily Hever, still in prison uniform, sat on a bench as near as possible to Miss Harker's office, listening to what was going on. Since Norah's death, she was virtually without friends and spent much of her time trying to ingratiate herself with the screws, without any success. At the moment, Miss Harker was sitting behind her desk and Miss Parrish was standing, obviously annoyed and very much on her dignity.

'Even though we have been forced to share this Wing,' she was saying, 'I am responsible for the women in my care.'

'Of course,' replied Janet.

'That goes for the ones who are having to double up with your women.'

'No,' said Janet, 'I can't agree to that.'

'Why not?'

'No-one would know who is in charge.'

Janet Harker hoped she put sufficient authority in her voice and that Martha Parrish did not sense how scared she was. 'We are two separate units,' she went on bravely. 'I wouldn't presume to tell you how to run yours.'

'I should hope not!' said Miss Parrish.

It was unfortunate that just at that moment Faye should appear in the doorway.

'Not interrupting, am I?'

'Miss Parrish and I were discussing how the Wing is to be reorganised while we are sharing.'

'Can I help?' said Faye.

Martha Parrish spoke very stiffly. 'It appears to be settled, Governor. Miss Harker has made her position very clear. If you'll excuse me, I have work to do.' With a disagreeable look, she left.

'Oh dear!' said Faye.

'She wants the women locked in when they're not working.'

Faye was irritated.

'But the whole point of doing this work was to give the extra space so that they needn't spend hours locked in. I'll have to call an Assistant Governors meeting. We can talk it all out then.' She saw Lily Hever sitting nearby and shut the door. 'Are the women still ostracising Lily?'

'On the whole, yes. She's never been popular.'

'I hate to write her off, but it's hard to see what one can do to help her.'

'She had a lovely time creating panic in the new wings,' said Janet.

'In what way?'

'She let it get around that the reason for the alterations was to give the women more floor space to clean, and so more hours spent on cleaning fatigue. Many of them believed it. It took me quite a while to convince them that the filling-in had been entirely for their own good. She's an aggravating woman. And a wicked one, too.'

'I'm afraid so,' said Faye. There was a moment's pause, as they both thought of Norah. Then Faye opened the door and said, 'I must go and see how they are getting on in the South Wing. The sooner they are finished, the better you will be pleased. For some reason the work seems to be slowing up a bit.'

When Faye came out, Lily half rose eagerly.

'Why madam –' she said. As usual she wanted to get into the Governor's good books. But Faye only smiled briefly and passed on.

Lily remained brooding on her bench. So madam didn't want to talk to her. Never mind. She'd show madam. For Lily had a very shrewd suspicion that something was up on South Wing. Yesterday she had watched the cleaning party leave, escorted by Officer Roberts. It had consisted of three women, Fran (whom Lily avoided as much as possible), Valerie, the fair-haired girl with the angelic face, and another woman of Lily's own age, a new admission. Before they left the Wing, Lily had noticed that Fran had been talking to Margie Bassett. Margie had cheered up for a bit, but now she seemed very down again. Yesterday she had given something to Fran as they left and Fran had tucked it down the front of the T-shirt she was wearing. A fag perhaps, thought Lily, intrigued by this.

Later in the morning, when the cleaning detail came back, Lily was on the look out. Her curiosity was rewarded. Fran came up the stairs last. She went straight to Margie who was standing in her cell door, tense, obviously waiting and gave her a piece of paper wrapped round a cigarette.

Margie gave the cigarette to Fran, and then read her note, avidly. She was beginning to break down; she turned and went into her cell.

What was up? Had Margie got a fella? Fran had moved away, talking and joking with some other women. She had lit her cigarette and was inhaling luxuriously. Lily sidled up to Margie's cell. The girl was reading the crumpled note again, there were tears in her eyes.

Lily paused in the doorway.

'Well, well, well,' she said.

Margie looked up, surprised and startled.

'What is it?' she said.

Lily crept further into the cell.

'You got a fella? Sending you notes, is he?'

Margie summoned up her courage.

'It's none of your business,' she said.

'Maybe not. But if you've got something going there –' Lily paused. Margie was scared.

'What're you after?' she asked.

'I just thought – you wouldn't like the screws to find out, eh? Maybe you've got something fixed up, trying to have a bit, eh? I don't blame you, duckie.'

'It's not like that,' she said.

'No?' Lily didn't believe her.

'He's my husband,' said Margie. 'He's Joe.'

Lily was surprised and delighted at the possibilities this news conjured up.

'Well,' she said, 'That makes it all the more important, don't it?'

Margie looked up. Seeing the look on Lily's face, she realised she had done a very stupid thing.

Unfortunately for Lily, Fran came back at that moment and saw Lily in Margie's cell.

'What are you doing here?' she asked fiercely.

Lily cringed. She was terrified of Fran. 'Just talking,' she said.

'What do you want?' Fran looked threatening.

'Nothing,' Lily sidled past her out of the door and dived into her own cell.

'Creep!' said Fran.

'She knows about Joe,' said Margie.

'Don't worry luv. I'll see she keeps her mouth shut,' said Fran. She sat next to Margie on the bottom bunk and talked very quietly. 'It's OK for tomorrow,' she said. 'I've found a place. Now listen, this is what you've got to do . . .' and Margie listened avidly as her tough friend told her the plan.

The next day on South Wing the Governor stood watching the confusion she had helped to create. Scaffolding rose round the girders to the height of the second floor. The empty centre office was being used to store bricks. A ladder, too, was there, reaching up to the first floor. Near the ladder two men were mixing cement on a large square of wood. A third, Joe Bassett, was taking a hod of bricks up the ladder to the first floor. Beyond him other men were working on the scaffolding. They consisted of a party of about twenty men from Cricklewood under the charge of two male officers and a foreman officer. Everywhere there was chaos and noise. Men were whistling as they worked; instructions were being shouted, and there was dust – dust everywhere. Faye knew she was wasting time but she could not resist watching. Her dream was coming true.

She was joined by Charles Radley.

'I can hardly believe it,' she said.

'It's coming on pretty well,' he answered.

'The difference it's going to make.'

Radley was not quite as enthusiastic as Faye. He knew there were bound to be personality problems. Indeed, they had started already.

A party of women prisoners carrying their mops and pails passed them. Among them were Fran, Valerie and Margie. They said good morning to Faye and went on to report to the small office by the main doors, where a principal officer was on duty. Mrs Armitage came down the spiral stairs towards them.

'I told the Works Officer you wanted to see him, she said.

'Thanks, Chief.'

'There's something else madam.'

'Yes?'

'There seems to be a bit of trouble on North Wing.'

'Nothing's been reported,' said Faye. 'Have you spoken to Miss Harker?'

Mrs Armitage stiffened. 'She says she hasn't noticed anything.'

'I see. We must have a meeting and discuss this,' said Faye briskly. She turned and, with Radley, made her way back to her office, through the main doors.

Joe, with his hod of bricks was again at the foot of the ladder. He was a husky, good-looking man in his middle twenties. As he went towards the centre for more bricks, Fran came towards him.

'Where are you going?' called Mrs Armitage.

'I left my pail, Chief,' called Fran.

'Then get it quick. You're keeping the others waiting.'

There was a sudden clatter as a man above dropped some bricks. Mrs Armitage looked up to see what had happened. Fran seized her chance and flicked a folded piece of paper toward Joe, who picked it up quickly and slid it between two bricks on the hod. He began to climb the ladder again.

Fran took her pail from the corner where she had deliberately left it, and quickly rejoined the others. 'That worked all right,' she thought.

As Joe reached the top of the ladder, he quickly pushed the note into the front of his overalls. From above he watched as the main gate was unlocked and the women on cleaning duty were let through. Mrs Armitage went with them.

'Get on now,' she was saying, 'I won't have the dirt from here tramped into the other wings.'

She went to have a word with the duty officer, her back was turned. Margie looked up. She and Joe exchanged a long look. Then, as Mrs Armitage turned, Margie bent and made a great show of cleaning the floor.

In her office, Faye was talking to Radley.

'I wish Mrs Armitage didn't see trouble everywhere.'

'She has got a nose for it,' he said.

'It can be valuable,' Faye agreed, 'but I wish she wasn't so biased against Janet Harker.'

'Janet Harker is young and wants to experiment. The Chief's whole outlook is different. You must make allowances, Faye.'

Faye smiled. 'I do. For both sides. No-one is right every time.'

There was a knock at the door and Henry Mackie, the Works Officer, came in.

'Ah, Mr Mackie,' said Faye. 'Sit down. I wanted to thank you for the way the work is going so far. How long will it take to finish?'

'South Wing? I'd say about five weeks.'

'As long as that? They did North Wing in three.'

'I know. But the rate of work has begun to slow down.'

'So I've noticed,' said Radley. 'Why is that?'

'Could be a variety of reasons.'

'Such as?' asked Faye.

'Well, we've lost two of our best men. They came up for release. We could hardly keep them in the pokey just because we wanted some building done.'

'Hardly,' said Radley smiling.

'It's a funny thing with working parties from inside,' said Mr Mackie, warming to his subject. 'Sometimes everything goes fine, no problems. Then – wham! – the standard falls off and you have to check and double check everything. Of course they may be going slow because they like it here. They're not locked up, they've a man's work to do and it's a change of scene.'

'I see,' said Faye. 'Anyhow do try and shorten those five weeks if you can. The women from South Wing are having to double up in other wings. It's causing a bit of tension.'

'I'll do what I can. I'll go and have a word with the foreman now,' said Mr Mackie, as he left with the Deputy Governor.

Faye told Penny to arrange for the Assistant Governors to come and see her. She remained at her desk.

'Penny,' she added, 'will you also ask Miss Harker to

send Peggy Abbott down tomorrow. She's due for discharge tomorrow and I want a word with her.'

'Yes, Mrs Boswell.'

The next day, when Peggy arrived she was beaming. Faye felt she was almost too happy and excited and only hoped that things would go well for this girl. She tried to impress on her the absolute necessity of being a good mother.

'Now you have been taught by Sister, you know how to look after your babies.'

'Oh yes, madam, I do.'

At last Peggy was talking more fluent English. 'And if ever you want to go out dancing, you must choose an evening when your aunt can babysit. You must not leave them alone ever, whilst they are so young. Do you understand?'

'I understand,' said Peggy.

'Give my respects to your uncle. He has been very good to you. you know.'

'Yes, madam I know.'

Her eyes were gleaming with excitement and anticipation as she spoke. Faye realised that she had entirely forgotten how much she had suffered. Forgotten as a child forgets. It had left no impression on her. Would she remember this homily? Faye doubted it.

'Well goodbye, Peggy, and good luck.'

'Goodbye lady – I mean madam. You come and visit me, perhaps, and see my babies?'

'I'd love to, Peggy, when you are settled in.'

As Peggy fairly danced from the room, Faye smiled and gave her head a little shake. How she hoped that Peggy would not be back in Stone Park within a year or two. But she would not have bet against it.

Faye rang through and asked Penny Hayes to bring any personal letters which she had had this morning. It was amazing how many of the discharged prisoners wrote after they had left. This morning there was a rather illiterate scrawl from old Mrs Weekes. It said she was happy looking after her sister who was now a semi-invalid. Could the Welfare lady look in when she had time, she wanted to ask her advice? And remember her to one and all at Stone Park, how sad to read of poor little Norah's death and she hoped Madam was well and she was hers respectfully (Mrs) Georgina Weekes.

The second letter was written on white paper so stiff that it almost stood up by itself. It was from Clive Benedict, Sally's father. He wondered if Mr and Mrs Boswell would care to dine with him at the Dorchester one day next week. The letter had obviously been written by, not dictated to, a high-powered secretary and was couched in unconsciously condescending terms. No, thought Faye, Mr and Mrs Boswell would not care to. Mr. Boswell was in Canada for three more weeks and Mrs Boswell had more than enough on her hands. Then she saw that the sting was in the tail, or rather in the postscript which had obviously been written by Benedict himself.

'P.S. I would like to ask your advice over Sally. I have offered her a London boutique, and a race horse of her own, but she is insistent that she wants to go and do community work in Bangladesh for three years. It seems a waste of her gifts. I know she now has a great admiration for you and that you might be able to dissuade her.'

So that's it! Good for you, Sally, thought Faye. It will give you all the challenge you need and will rid you of a lot of your half-baked ideas. It meant that she would have to decide to meet him some time, for she could not refuse the opportunity to help Sally. She would answer this letter herself, from home. At least she reflected, Sally had achieved her object in drawing her father's attention to her. Though at the time it had seemed a somewhat extreme remedy.

The third letter was from Beth Radley, a stilted little note in good handwriting, thanking her for the dinner Faye had given them the week before, on the eve of Bill's departure. It was polite of her to write, thought her hostess, as she had obviously not wanted to come. Fortunately,

Faye had invited another couple, a talkative executive from the BBC and his pretty wife, neither of whom had any interest at all in the Prison Service, which had no doubt given Charles Radley, who was interested in not-thing else, a dull evening. But Beth had lost her tight expression and had laughed and enjoyed herself. Watching her, Faye had thought how frustrating it must be for Beth to be married to this good-looking man who could never leave his work behind him. He was utterly dedicated and should never have married. At Stone Park he had once or twice proved himself invaluable in awkward or even dangerous situations, where Faye could not have coped nearly as well. Such as when the women staged a two-day hunger strike and literally all food was sent away untouched. And another time when a hysterical prisoner managed to get on to the roof and refused to come down, In each case the fact that he was a man, and therefore able to approach women from a man's angle, had helped to solve the problem. He also could talk to the rougher women in their own language without forfeiting their respect. But none of these qualities made him a better husband to Beth. Faye wished she knew him well enough to talk to him about this. Faye did not flatter herself that she was never guilty of taking her work home. Bill had been an angel of patience during her first months at Stone Park, when she had sometimes felt swamped by the problems that came up. But they had a full outside life as well. On Faye's days off they invariably went to the theatre or dined with friends and, at weekends when she was free, they went out into the country or to concerts. Still, she must be careful when Bill came back not to swamp him with her Stone Park problems.

She shut her correspondence file and went down to South Wing again. She was interested to find out what was holding up the work.

She went through the main door and locked them behind her. She was soon joined by Mr Mackie and by Harry, the foreman officer.

'Good day madam,' he said to Faye.

'How's it coming on?' said Mackie.

'Slowly. They look as if they are working but nothing much gets done.'

'Can't you ginger them up?' asked Mackie.

'That's easier said, Mr Mackie. I don't know what's got into them.'

'Do your best, Harry,' said Faye. 'If we could say with some certainty that this work will be finished in three weeks, it would be a great relief.'

'It won't be for want of trying, madam' said Mackie. 'But just now it seems to be one thing after another. Yesterday, rungs in the ladder were unsafe and I had to send for a new one.'

'And this morning there was too much sand in the cement,' added Harry. 'If I hadn't spotted it we'd have had to tear down a whole section of the wall and start again.'

'Can it be deliberate?' asked Faye.

'I don't see how, madam. The men are all good workers, though maybe a bit careless.'

'Well,' said Faye, 'do what you can and you'll earn my eternal gratitude.'

She and Mackie turned away and went back through the main doors, while Harry went up the ladder again.

A few minutes later the cleaning party was crossing the Centre preparatory to going into the Admin. Corridor. Fran was thankful to see that Mrs Armitage was no longer with them: she had eyes like a hawk, and the plan which Fran had thought out had much more chance of success if the Chief were not about.

Under the scaffolding, beyond the bricks, lengths of timber were stacked against the wall, forming a corner hidden from the rest of the centre. Fran glanced quickly up. Joe was no longer standing at the top of the ladder and another man was now taking the hod of bricks up. Fran looked at one of the other prisoners who was mixing cement, and gave him a signal. He nodded. A moment later, he gave a loud curse and stepped back on his pail, with the result that cement was split everywhere. The cleaning party screamed and moved away to avoid being splashed by it. The foreman officer hurried down the ladder. Mrs Roberts rushed over to see what had happened.

Immediately Fran added to the general confusion by making a great commotion, shouting loudly and rushing here and there. She continued this until she saw that Margie had managed to slip away, unnoticed, to the safe haven of Joe's arms, hidden behind the timbers.

CHAPTER FOURTEEN

Margie and Joe half-lay, half-sat on the dusty floor. They were in a private world behind the pile of timber, a thousand light years away from Stone Park Prison. They held each other fiercely, as though they could never let go. They talked in whispers.

'Joe, oh Joe,' Margie was saying.

'I was too quick then, love,' Joe was saying. 'No good for you. Better next time.'

'Just to have you again, Joe. I don't know how I've stood it.'

'Me, too.'

'When the building's finished and you go . . . being separated again. It'll be awful.'

'Don't worry. We've got days yet. The lads are stretching it all they can. They all think you're a smashing girl, they do. Envy me, proper.'

Margie giggled.

'They like the big dark bird, too.' Joe added.

'Fran? She fancies one of the chaps. Wants a bit. She's the one who planned everything. We share a cell.'

Joe scowled and strained her closer to him.

'You're not getting to be a les, are you?' he asked, instantly jealous.

Margie laughed.

'Don't be silly, Joe. You know me – oh, love I can't believe it. It's really you. When I saw you that first day. I nearly fainted.'

'I knew I'd see you when I heard I was on the working party. Couldn't write or warn you.'

'Course not,' said Margie. She was kissing him as she spoke, gentle soft kisses over his face and neck, and touching him too. It was all too much for Joe.

'Must have you again love,' he said. Come on.'

'S'posing they find us?'

'Let 'em,' said Joe recklessly.

Mrs Armitage had gone up to South Wing to have a word with Miss Parrish about some transfers tomorrow. She found her colleague in a bad temper and who could blame her. During the alterations the place was like a bear garden. Women playing ping-pong, women watching television, and squabbling over which channel to have, women arguing, talking, laughing. No doubt 'Madam' thought this was a very relaxed atmosphere. Mrs Armitage could not agree. She longed for the old days back again.

Someone tugged at her sleeve. She looked round. It was Lily Hever, as furtive as ever. The Chief wanted to throw her off and walk away, but that would not do. Prisoners must be listened to.

'What is it, Lily?' she said hoping her dislike would not show in her voice, and added sharply, 'Why aren't you on cleaning fatigue?'

'It's me leg,' said Lily. 'I saw Dr Ward yesterday and he said –'

'Spare me the details,' said the Chief and thought to herself. 'Dr Ward – he's the young one who was so certain poor Norah would live. Good thing he's leaving. If it had been Dr Mayes now –' Aloud she said, even more sharply, 'Well, what is it?'

'Only wanted to pass the time of day, Chief. Nobody talks to me much now.'

'That's no-one's fault but your own, Lily.' Mrs Armitage had satisfaction in saying this. She was about to pass on when Lily said;

'Funny about Joe, isn't it madam?'

Mrs Armitage stopped.

'Joe? Who's Joe?'

'Joe Bassett. Margie's husband. On this wing. Funny he should be one of the working party. Someone must've made a mistake somewhere, eh?'

'I don't know what you're talking about,' said Mrs Armitage and strode away.

'Don't you? You silly old bugger,' thought Lily. She smiled in a satisfied way. She had injected her poison. Now let it work.

Mrs Armitage went straight to Faye's office. When she came in Faye started rather guiltily. She had been playing truant for a few minutes. Overcome by a sudden longing to talk to Bill, she had been writing him a letter instead of checking the morning's arrivals. She hastily covered the letter with a file and greeted Mrs Armitage warmly. She did feel that at last they were beginning to have a better relationship.

'What is it?' she said.

'I think I've found out the answer to the slowing down of the work,' said Mrs Armitage.

'Good for you. What is it?'

'It was deliberate. One of the prisoners from Cricklewood is Joe Bassett, Margie Bassett's husband. She's on North Wing.'

Faye was incredulous.

'Are you sure?'

'Quite sure.'

Faye took out the typed list of the men prisoners which she had been given and ran her finger down it.

'Yes, here it is. Joe Bassett, twenty-five, three years for car thefts.' She looked up. 'He was a mechanic who tried to set up on his own by selling stolen cars.'

'Yes,' said the Chief.

'And what's his wife's offence?'

'She got six months for receiving,' said Mrs Armitage.

'So that's it. All the other men were in on this. They were deliberately slowing down, to give them more time together.'

'That's it, madam.'

'How long has it been going on?'

'Several days, I should imagine.'

'Well, it must stop.' Faye's tone was almost regretful. 'I must say I take off my hat to them – under our noses.'

'This building has caused a lot of confusion. Everything's at sixes and sevens,' said Mrs Armitage defending her colleagues.

'Exactly, so the sooner we get the work going again, the better. We'd better have Mr Radley with us. She rose. 'Come along Chief.'

In their haven, Joe was whispering to Margie as he ran his hands up and down her body,

'I've got another eighteen months, even with remission. Don't know how I'll stand it.'

'You'll stand it, love. I'll be out soon and I'll visit whenever I'm allowed to.'

'How'll you manage?'

'I'll get a job and a room near you. The Welfare Officers will help. They're good about that in here.'

'They should never have nicked you. You didn't even know that car was hot.'

'They didn't believe that. Joe, promise you'll go straight when you come out?'

But Joe didn't reply to this.

A sudden instinct made her say,

'Kiss me Joe. Quick.'

As he held her tightly, she heard voices outside and then Harry saying loudly,

'Come along, Bassett, break it up.'

And then Faye's voice,

'Give them a moment, Harry.'

Joe grinned bitterly.

'She's afraid we're at it,' he said.

Margie straightened her skirt, resigned.

'Bye love,' she said and flung her arms round him for a long kiss. Then they stepped out. Joe suddenly felt he would like to kill them all, standing there watching him and Margie. He stood belligerently in front of her.

'Don't try anything,' said Charles Radley, sharply. 'Don't be a bloody fool, Bassett.'

And Mrs Armitage said firmly, but not unkindly,

'Come along, Mrs Bassett.'

Lily was terrified. News travels fast in prison, and already Miss Harker had heard from a prison officer what had happened. Any minute now the cleaning fatigue would be back and with them, Fran. She remembered what Fran had said to her two days ago. 'You shop Margie and I'll do you. I'll fix you so your own mum wouldn't know you.' She meant it too.

Mrs Armitage came up with Margie who was sobbing. The Chief took her to her cell and went to speak to Miss Harker. Lily had moved as far as possible away, the whole length of the wing, near the blocked in staircase. She suddenly realised what a foolish thing she had done for they were all coming back up the stairs and Fran was leading them. Lily turned and ran screaming.

'I didn't shop her! I didn't! Honest I didn't!'

Fran was running faster. She will catch me thought Lily and then what'll I do?

Like a hunted hare she bolted for sanctuary into Miss Harker's office. Mrs Armitage, seeing the women pelting after her, realised the situation and banged the door shut almost in Fran's furious face.

Lily was panting.

'That Fran. She'll do me.'

'It's all you deserve, Lily,' said the Chief, and added to Miss Harker, 'She'd better ask for Rule 43.'

Neither Janet nor Lily were with her.

'What is that?' asked Janet, who had not come across this situation before.

'Prisoner confined to her cell at her own request.'

Lily could have embraced Mrs Armitage.

'Yes, I remember now,' she said. 'Know me rights. I can be shut in by myself if I want to.'

'For her own protection,' said Mrs Armitage and added to Janet, quietly, 'And for the sake of peace and quiet in the wing.'

'Very well, Lily. If that's what you really wish.'

'Will you give me a minute, Miss Harker. If Lily could stay in here?'

'Of course.' At this moment, Janet had complete confidence in the Chief.

Mrs Armitage opened the door and as quickly shut it behind her. A group of sullen-looking women stood facing her. In front stood Fran, glowering and very dangerous. Mrs Armitage knew that she was at risk. This woman would not hesitate to do to her what that devil had done to poor Ted all those years ago. The very thought of that made her angry and her anger lent her strength, a strength which Fran recognised.

'Come along Fran,' she said. 'Into your cell and cool off.'

Amazingly, recognising true authority, Fran obeyed. Quickly Mrs Armitage motioned to another officer to lock her in.

'And if the Governor gives me a reprimand for this,' she thought, 'I'll hand in my resignation.'

She went over to the women,

'Go along to recess and clean yourselves up,' she said shortly, and watched them shuffle away.

From Margie came heartbroken sobs. From Fran, silence. Soon it would be roars, clatters from a tin plate, and banging on the door until Fran had got it out of her system.

The chief went to the office. Together, she and Janet escorted Lily to her cell to be locked in at her own request.

As they left her, Miss Harker said,

'I haven't met this rule before.'

'It's not often observed.'

'It must mean a lot of work. Taking in meals, escorting her to recess.'

'It'll be worth it for a while, until Fran cools down. She's a tough customer and we don't want a murder in the prison,' said Mrs Armitage.

'Lily's still got a year to serve. She'll have to come out before then.'

In her cell Lily, shaking, was thinking just that thing. One day, inevitably, she would have to come out and face Fran.

The next day at Disciplinary, Margie came up before Faye. She stood in front of the desk, her normally pretty face swollen with crying. Fayes voice was stern.

'You've heard the charge. Have you anything to say?'

Margie shook her head.

'No madam,' she whispered.

'You have broken a very strict rule, Mrs Bassett. However, I am not so concerned with how often you met your husband, nor what took place, as with the fact that because of you, your husband talked or bribed the rest of his working party into going slow and holding up essential work in this prison. That could have had far more serious consequences. On the other hand, I realise that the temptation must have been very great, and that you were unable to resist this opportunity of being together. I have taken it into account and, if it were not for this, your punishment would be more severe. Seven days loss of pay and privileges.'

Margie gasped. She had not expected anything so lenient.

Mrs Armitage gave an approving nod. Faye lent forward speaking in a different voice, with compassion and sympathy.

'Now that may seem very light – but your real punishment will be to know that every man on that working party will be disciplined. The Governor of their prison takes a very serious view, and I'm afraid that your husband is bound to lose some of his remission.'

Margie gazed at Faye, stricken, unable to believe it. She was led away sobbing, by the officer and Mrs Armitage.

Radley, who had been watching all this, rose.

'I'll go and see Mackie,' he said, 'I gather that we'll have our work party back tomorrow, minus Joe Bassett, and this time it will be full-speed ahead.'

'Yes,' said Faye, and added, 'I do feel sorry for Margie Bassett.'

'So do I in a way,' said Radley.

'No,' said Faye. 'Completely. I have every sympathy

for her. I know that if I were ever in her circumstances, with a chance to see my husband, I'd do exactly the same.'

In Faye's office a meeting was taking place. The two Assistant Governors were sitting facing each other. Neither looked particularly happy. Faye was wearing what Bill would have called 'her Governor's face'. She was tired of the constant friction between these two women. She was even more tired of the fight that Martha Parrish was putting up in order to keep things just as they were. At the same time, she could not let Janet Harker feel she could 'cheek' Miss Parrish with impunity, for the older woman was her senior officer and inter-staff discipline must be maintained.

'I hope I have made myself sufficiently clear. There will be no more locked cells in this prison except during the hours of darkness and in specific cases.'

Miss Parrish felt obliged to interrupt.

'But Mrs Boswell—' she started to protest. Faye stopped her.

'I know,' she said, 'that to many of the staff a regimented clockwork prison with everything done by numbers is still the ideal.'

'It makes for peace and quiet madam,' said Miss Parrish, determined to have her say.

'Quite. What it does not do is help the women to be better citizens when they come out. The more recent theory is that prisoners should be given an element of choice – even of self-government.'

'Self-government!' Miss Parrish muttered beneath her breath.

'I like that idea,' said Janet Harker enthusiastically.

'So do I,' it was the Governor speaking again. 'Unfortunately, I am afraid that the majority of the prisoners are not ready for it. Now, to return to the locked doors. The women, now there is room to roam, will have more freedom of movement on their own landings. It is a system that is working well on North Wing despite the present overcrowding, and when South Wing is finished, it will be extended to there.'

Miss Parrish was tense.

'Is that an order Governor?'

Faye looked at her.

'I hope it won't be necessary to make it one, Miss Parrish.'

'Now, if you'll excuse me—' said Janet Harker and left, for she had a shrewd suspicion that Faye wanted a word alone with Miss Parrish. In this she was perfectly right. Faye opened a drawer in her desk and took out a large portfolio.

'I wanted to thank you for what you did for Norah,' she said.

'I did no more than was necessary,' said Martha. 'As far as I was concerned, she was a model prisoner.'

'I didn't mean on the Wing, I meant in hospital. I only heard the other day, when I went there to see that appendix case from Remand, that you had sat with her through the night when she was dying. It is good to know she had someone she loved with her when she died.'

'She didn't "love" me, Governor,' said Martha in a tight, constrained voice.

'She did, you know. I had a long talk with her that day before Lily Hever got hold of her again. It was your day off I think. She seemed much less withdrawn. She spoke a lot of you and showed me some drawings she had made of you. I thought they were remarkably good. And as I left she said, "I never knew my mum, but I think she must have been just like Miss Parrish" – so I wanted to tell you how thankful I was to know that you were with her that last night.'

'Thank you,' Miss Parrish spoke gruffly. She rose quickly and went to the window where she stood staring out. For Martha Parrish, so controlled, so self-possessed, was fighting back her tears.

After a moment, Faye spoke in a deliberately lighter tone.

'You know,' she said, 'that when the building is all finished we hope to have an exhibition of prisoners' work. I thought it would be nice to have some of Norah's drawings there. Perhaps you would like to take the portfolio and chose what you'd like to show. And as she had no named next of kin, maybe you would like to keep the rest for yourself.'

A pause. Miss Parrish was under control again.

'Thank you. I'd like that.'

She turned and came towards the desk to take the portfolio. She saw a photograph of Paul on the desk.

'Your son, isn't it?' she asked. 'The officers were raving over his looks. How is he?'

'Having a wonderful time. Crewing for a tycoon, sailing round the Mediterranean. Doing what he likes best and getting well paid for it, lucky boy.'

'I envy him,' and a brief smile lightened her whole face.

'Do you sail?' Faye asked.

A blind was again drawn over Martha's face.

'I did – once,' she said briefly. 'Now I'd better go. Not that Miss Harker isn't perfectly capable—' At the door she turned and said, 'Although I don't entirely agree, Governor, I do take your point about the locked doors,' and still unsmiling, left.

For a moment the Governor pondered. What a sad, enigmatic woman she was. What had happened to make her so? Faye knew of Martha's friendship with one of the long-term prisoners in South Wing, she had been told of it by her predecessor, in deepest confidence, and had never mentioned it to a soul. This would have horrified the Assistant Governor, who thought her secret was carefully guarded. But now the Home Office was considering transferring the woman in question to an open prison in the North and as it was a matter of policy, Faye might not be able to prevent it happening. If it did happen, she thought, it might be more than Martha Parrish could bear.

CHAPTER FIFTEEN

Faye had been away for a holiday with her husband. For the whole of her first year at Stone Park and longer, she had refused to take more than the odd day off. After she had been there for over eighteen months, Bill had lost his temper and insisted that she took a three-week holiday, which she badly needed.

They motored to Provence, where they stayed at a comfortable, typically French hotel in a medieval hill village about five miles from the coast.

After the first week Faye relaxed completely. They drove down to Port Grimaud where they had friends who owned a boat; they took picnics on the maquis where they sat with the sweep of the purple-grey mountains behind them, and the vast sea as still as a lake below; where the air was vibrant with the hum of bees and the chirp of crickets and the smell of thyme and sage filled their nostrils. In the evenings they ate delicious food on a terrace with a far reaching view.

They drove home by easy stages, visiting an occasional cathedral, for Bill's pleasure, and looking at châteaux for Faye's. It was in every way a most satisfactory holiday.

On their return, they both felt that they had been away for three months, rather than weeks. Even a message from Bill's office, asking if he could go at once to Brussels, had not seemed irritating.

When he left the next morning Faye kissed him goodbye, 'It was a marvellous holiday,' she said. 'Thank you, Bill.'

The uniformed man on the gate greeted her like a long lost friend.

'Good to see you back, madam,' he said. 'We've missed you.'

On the way to her office she was greeted by many

smiles, and stopped to have several chats; as a result it took longer than usual to reach her office. On her desk was a bunch of mixed flowers.

'Where did they come from?' she asked Penny Halewood who had greeted her with a beaming face.

'From our garden,' said Penny. 'To welcome you back.'

'How nice of you, Penny,' said Faye. 'How is your mother?'

'Her arm's a lot better,' said Penny. And added, 'I got your postcard. Did you have a wonderful holiday, Mrs Boswell?'

'Marvellous,' said Faye and wished to herself it wasn't over. She started to go through her mail. She looked up, but Penny was still hovering.

'Did you want anything, Penny?' she asked.

'Mr Radley wanted to see you as soon as you came in,' answered Penny.

That sounds ominous, thought Faye and said aloud, 'Tell him to come along as soon as he likes.'

She started to look at the list of admissions whilst she way away. Thirty women had been discharged and thirty-three admitted. The prison population remained fairly constant. Miss Parrish was on leave and Miss Flaxton was acting as Assistant Governor for South Wing. In the Remand Wing – but she got no further than this when Charles Radley came in. Faye was pleased to see him.

' 'Morning Charles,' she said.

'Good morning, Faye. You look wonderfully well.'

'I feel it,' said Faye. 'Have you settled your holiday yet?'

'We can't agree where to go.'

'You'd better hurry up, your leave starts next month. Now, what's the worry?'

Radley was holding one of the smaller daily papers, a tabloid, folded open at the second page.

'Have you seen the papers today?' he said.

'Not yet.'

'Well, perhaps you'd better read this,' said Radley and

laid the folded paper on the desk. On it was a photograph of a girl, Mary Kyle, and a headline in heavy type: 'Gun-girl Mary wastes away in prison'. Faye's post-holiday mood rapidly left her as she read: 'The health of Mary Kyle, aged 27, remanded in custody at Stone Park Prison, was said yesterday to be causing concern. Miss Kyle, a self-styled revolutionary, is charged with complicity in the raid on Beech Street Magistrates' Court in which an attempt was made to force the release of accused urban guerrilla leader, Norman Lipsky.'

Faye looked up.

'Was that the raid where one policeman was killed and another injured?' she asked.

'Yes,' said Radley. 'She's charged with smuggling the guns in to the men.'

'But this is only a rehash of the original reports,' said Faye.

'It's the end of the article that's important.'

Faye looked at the paper again.

'Her solicitor, Leo Stenhill, claims that she has lost nearly a stone in weight over the last five weeks.'

Faye was worried to read this. She thought, ruefully, that she should not have gone on holiday. She went on reading.

'Mary Kyle is showing signs of nervous exhaustion. "I have no doubt that excessive strictness and the active animosity of the prison staff are the direct cause," Mr Stenhill told our reporter.'

Faye put down the paper.

'Has there been anything about this in the medical report? Let's see it.'

Radley handed her the file.

'Obviously none of the medical staff think it's as serious as it's made out in that article,' he said.

'But, I presume she did lose weight when she was first here,' answered Faye, looking at the file.

Radley shrugged. 'That's a common phenomenon amongst prisoners on remand, especially for the first time.'

'I know,' said Faye. 'That's what Peter Mayes seems to have concluded. She lost five, nearly six pounds – but by her examination last week, it appears to have stopped.'

'So she exaggerated it to her solicitor, and he passed it on,' said Radley.

'Apparently. You've seen the Kyle girl. What do you think of her?'

'She's rather antagonistic, very self-assured. Certainly not nervous.'

'She can't expect to work up much sympathy for herself by a story that can be so easily disproved,' said Faye. 'At least it's only appeared in one paper so far. If any of the others want to take it up, we can give them the facts.'

'Mary Kyle is a very unlikely martyr,' said Radley. 'Still, I'm glad the Chief Officer mentioned it to me.'

'So am I,' said Faye. And she thought to herself, 'So we are going to have trouble with the press.'

As soon as she had dealt with her correspondence, Faye sent for Mrs Armitage who arrived carrying a book.

'Hullo, Mrs Armitage,' said Faye. 'I'm sorry to hear all this about Mary Kyle.'

'I'm sorry you've come back to trouble,' said the Chief. 'I took the liberty of sending for this.'

'What is it? Ah, the Refused Food book.'

'Yes. Mr Radley signed it in your absence. You will see that on the 4th, 7th and 12th, the Kyle girl is marked as having refused one or more major meals.'

'So I see,' said Faye.

'And in the first week she was on remand – whilst you were away – she refused food entirely over two twenty-four hour periods, and was seen by the Medical Officer. That goes some way to explain the loss of weight mentioned in the newspaper article.'

'It's worrying,' said Faye.

'There's the other thing as well, madam.'

'What's that?'

'Her solicitor implied that she is being ill-treated. I

suggest we interview the girl and the officer concerned at once. If necessary, we could have an inquiry.'

Privately Faye thought Mrs Armitage was jumping the gun.

'Aren't you perhaps making a little too much of it? I'm seeing the girl, of course, this morning.'

Mrs Armitage spoke stiffly.

'I'm not so concerned about the girl as about the officers on my staff.'

'Why? No accusation has been made,' said Faye.

'With respect, Madam – I've seen this before. A rumour of bad treatment starts. There are always some prisoners who take advantage of it. We should crack down now, before it gets out of hand.'

Faye remembered how obstinate the Chief could be. 'Sorry, but I have no intention of "cracking down",' she answered firmly.

Mrs Armitage tried again. 'As I see it, prison can only function in an atmosphere of strict discipline. Once that is relaxed, you are bound to have trouble.'

'She is back in her old belligerent mood,' thought Faye. 'And we had been getting on so much better.' Aloud she said firmly, 'I don't agree Mrs Armitage, and I hope you won't encourage this kind of thinking.'

She handed the Refused Food book back to the Chief who took it, with pursed lips. Try as she would, she could not come round to the Governor's way of thinking.

Faye glanced at the Admissions Book.

'I'll have to go round with you and meet the new people,' she said.

'We've an old friend back with us,' said Mrs Armitage.

'Who's that?'

'Mrs Weekes.'

'Oh no! And Miss Clarke took so much trouble over her. Shoplifting again I suppose?'

'Of course.'

'Wasn't her sister an invalid?'

'Yes. Miss Clarke went round to their Local Authority

as soon as old Georgie came in. The sister's gone into a home.'

'Silly old thing. Old Georgie, I mean. Not the sister. Anyhow thank you for briefing me, Chief.'

'Any other news?' asked Faye.

'You know Fran was transferred, of course. That was arranged before your holiday. Well, a week later Lily Hever asked to come out of her cell. So there she is back on the wing again. Large as life and a perfect nuisance. Old Mrs Weekes won't talk to her, because of poor Norah. And Margie Bassett has gone. I believe Miss Clarke found her a job near Cricklewood. The prison, I mean.'

'So now she can visit her Joe,' thought Faye. Aloud she said, 'I'd better see this Kyle woman before anything else. Will you bring her along? I'd like you to be here.'

'Of course, madam—' at the door Mrs Armitage fired a parting shot. 'Oh, and Chef is giving in his notice. He wants to see you when you have time.'

'No!' Faye was dismayed. 'He's so jolly. All the women on kitchen detail love him. There's never any trouble there. And he's a good cook. Why's he leaving?'

'Going to work for a friend who has a hotel on the Costa Brava. He says he wants more scope. He's giving us three months before he leaves.'

'Thank you, Chief,' said Faye, with a woeful smile. 'That news has really made my day.'

For ten minutes she was alone. Then Mary Kyle arrived with the Chief and a prison officer escorting her. She was about twenty-seven years old, thin, pale, sharp featured, with long, fair hair. She wore a black jersey over skin tight black jeans tucked into knee-boots. She seemed completely indifferent to everything around her. She stood in front of the desk.

'Good morning, Mary,' said Faye.

'Yeah,' said Mary Kyle.

She spoke with a flat northern accent. Her attitude was one of barely concealed contempt.

Faye spoke to her in an impersonal way.

'Normally, I would have come to see you in the Remand Wing, but after the report in the paper this morning, I wanted to see you unofficially.'

Mary shrugged and said nothing.

Faye continued, 'The newspaper said that you have lost a considerable amount of weight. Nearly a stone. Have you?'

Mary still did not speak. Mrs Armitage shot her an angry look.

'The Chief Officer has pointed out that you have actually refused to eat on several occasions.'

Mary glanced at the Chief. At last she saw fit to speak.

'Yeah, I did at first, because the food was so godawful. But I take everything I can get now.'

'I'm going to ask the Doctor to put you on a special nutritional diet. The newspaper article also suggests that you feel you are being badly treated. Do you have any specific complaints?'

'It wouldn't do any good to tell you,' said Kyle.

'Why not?'

Kyle shrugged. 'If you're accused of killing a copper all the screws have got it in for you.'

As Faye knew there was some truth in this she did not comment. Mrs Armitage was getting tense.

'You won't help yourself by being offensive,' said Faye. 'In any case, while you are on remand, you are presumed innocent until proved guilty. You won't be treated any differently from anyone else.'

'That's a lot of talk. And you know it.'

Faye was angered by this.

'The rules here are simple. I'd advise you to co-operate with us.'

'Or what?' asked Mary.

'You are here waiting trial, not convicted. But you are still subject to prison discipline.'

'You bet,' said Mary.

There was a pause. Then she said,

'My solicitor's waiting to see me.'

'Very well,' said Faye. 'You can tell him that as soon as your interview is over, you are to report to the Medical Officer for a complete examination.'

Mary Kyle looked again at Mrs Armitage. She sneered faintly and went out with the officer. Mrs Armitage was seething.

'There are times when it's almost impossible to stay impartial,' she said in a taut voice.

'I agree. That one certainly makes it difficult.'

And for the first time that morning, the two women exchanged a smile.

Leo Stenhill was waiting for his client in a special interview cubicle. It was very small, just large enough for a table with two chairs on either side. The top half of the door and one wall were of glass, so that whoever was in the cubicle was in sight, but out of hearing. Mary Kyle's officer escort stood outside, watching through the glass. At the table inside, Mary was sitting opposite her solicitor. He was a smooth, short, deceptively quiet man in his forties. Kyle was talking vehemently, gesticulating.

'How would you like it? Cooped up in here with bloody screws watching you all the time!' she was saying. 'And that po-faced bitch of a Governor.'

'Not so loud!' said her lawyer. 'Now come on, take it easy. How can I discuss your defence with you, if you won't calm down?'

She did not, however, calm down, and their fifteen minute interview consisted mainly of vituperation against the screws from Mary. Leo Stenhill reflected that it was as well that they could not be overheard. To divert her, he said,

'I've some good news for you Mary. Victor Hartnoll, the M.P., may be taking your case up.'

'That phoney!'

Mr Stenhill was in agreement, but he did not tell her so.

'He could be a very valuable ally. If he sees you, mind

you impress him in the right way.' He glanced at his watch. 'Time is nearly up. I am going to see your Governor later this afternoon.'

'Her! If you ask me she doesn't know her arse from her elbow.'

But Mary was quite wrong, Faye was only too well aware of what was going on.

Mary was taken to the Hospital Wing where she was given a very thorough medical examination. After, Dr Mayes went straight to Faye's office where Mrs Armitage had been going through various books – Disciplinary, Letters Withheld, the Medicine Book and the like, in order to bring her up to date with the weeks she had missed. So much of a Governor's work consists of petty detail.

Faye could see that Doctor Mayes was very concerned over the woman he had just examined.

'It's damnable,' he said. 'She's lost just over a stone in all. That's nearly eight pounds loss since I examined her last week.'

Faye was shocked and startled by this.

'Why has it happened?' she asked.

'I don't yet know. I can't find anything medical to account for it.'

'The report says she went on hunger strike for two days. Could it be the result of that?' asked Faye.

'That was nearly three weeks ago. And she's been eating regularly since then. I've taken blood and urine samples. Perhaps they'll tell us something.'

'I thought she was exaggerating. What disturbs me is that she realised this was happening but didn't tell anyone except her solicitor,' said the Chief.

'I know. The press could make capital out of that – the fact that none of us noticed. And it could get worse.' She and Faye looked at each other.

'I must find out what's causing it,' said Dr Mayes.

Faye was silent, thinking this might lead to serious

trouble and she as Governor would be entirely responsible.

There was a knock on the door and Penny came in.

'Excuse me, madam,' she said, 'Mr Stenhill has arrived for his appointment.'

'All right, Penny.'

Penny went out.

Peter Mayes hesitated.

'I know him slightly. He's a tricky customer. I wouldn't exactly say he was dishonest but – may I suggest? – be careful?'

'I have no intention of discussing her case with him,' said Faye with some asperity. 'I shall only answer questions about her health or her welfare. And I'd appreciate it very much if you'd stay.'

'Certainly,' said Peter Mayes.

'I'd better be away, madam,' said Mrs Armitage nobly, for she was longing to stay. She did so for long enough to see for herself what Leo Stenhill was like. He was a small man with a ferret-like face. He came in smiling; always, he found, a safe opening gambit. At first sight he did not seem dangerous, but under his mild appearance lay a sharp, quick mind. At the moment, for his own purposes, he was diffident and almost apologetic.

'Good day, Mrs Boswell.'

Faye was extremely businesslike.

'Good day, Mr Stenhill. You've met Dr Mayes, the Senior Medical Officer?'

Stenhill smiled again.

'Oh, several times. How d'you do? I'm delighted you're here, Doctor.'

He turned to Faye. He appeared awkward, as if uncertain how to proceed. Faye thought, 'I believe he's putting on an act.' Aloud she said,

'Do sit down. Would you like some coffee?'

'Thank you, no. I don't want to take up too much of your time. I really came about that unfortunate article in the paper this morning. Did you—?'

'Yes,' said Faye. 'I saw it.'

'Perhaps I shouldn't have spoken to that reporter. But I was concerned about my client.'

'Naturally.'

Faye felt more relaxed. He did not seem as bad as she was led to believe. Rather a harmless sort of man. However, his next sentence caused her to change her mind.

'She tells me that she has had no real medical attention,' he said, looking at the Doctor.

'That is hardly the case. I have seen her each week and now I have put her on a high nutritional diet, and a course of vitamins,' answered Peter Mayes.

'Within the last hour?'

'Er – yes.'

'So you hadn't noticed her condition before today?'

Mr Stenhill sounded very smooth.

'Nothing was apparent at her last examination.'

'So you confirm that there has been a rapid and serious deterioration in Miss Kyle's condition?'

Faye listened, uneasily. When the Doctor spoke he sounded guarded.

'Well – there has been an appreciable loss of weight in a short period. But I don't know that I'd say it was serious or describe it as a "condition".'

'I see,' said Mr Stenhill. 'What do you think has caused it?'

'I'm not in a position to say.' The Doctor knew he was in potentially deep water.

'Isn't it a fact that mental stress can cause this sort of condition?' asked Mr Stenhill.

Faye thought it was time for her to speak.

'I don't believe that it has in this case,' she said. 'Nor do the psychiatrists who have seen her.'

'Why not, Mrs Boswell?' asked the lawyer in a deceptively casual manner.

'Here is her report.' She read from it. 'Kyle has shown no signs of undue stress. But she is unco-operative and generally keeps herself apart from the other remand prisoners. She has behaved well so far.'

Mr Stenhill jumped in on this.

'So far? How did you expect her to behave? And why are your officers so unsympathetic to her?'

His small eyes behind their glasses looked mean and his ferret-like nose seemed to twitch. Abruptly Faye lost her temper.

'In view of what she did, I think my officers would be more than human if they cared whether she was happy or not. Stone Park is not a holiday camp and discipline must be maintained.'

As soon as she had spoken she realised what a foolish thing she had said. The lawyer's eyes were gleaming but his manner when he spoke was still smooth and, Faye felt, utterly insincere.

'I am sorry if I have upset you, Mrs Boswell. I can only speak for what I see. The girl seems to me to have changed, to be nervous and indeed very frightened.'

Faye was on her guard now.

'She has a serious trial coming up,' she said.

'There's been so much bad publicity. In a case like this, there's very little sympathy for the accused. No doubt your officers read the newspapers?'

'I assure you it does not affect the way she is treated here. Doctor Mayes will confirm that.'

'Certainly,' said the Doctor stoutly.

'Must she be watched so strictly?' asked the lawyer. 'She tells me she is escorted everywhere, checked every hour of the night.'

'I needn't tell you, Mr Stenhill, that that is routine in the circumstances,' said Faye.

'And can you honestly say that your own attitude has not been influenced by those circumstances?'

'Yes, I can. Honestly. She is just a prisoner on remand. One of many.'

'But what about the officers in charge of her?'

Faye considered for a moment. He was now fishing a little too obviously.

'Whatever offence an inmate may be accused of, she is treated strictly according to how she behaves in prison.'

'Yes. Yes, of course.' There was a touch of sarcasm in Mr Stenhill's voice.

Faye rose. 'And that is as much as I am prepared to say.'

She pressed the call button on her desk. Stenhill realised that he was being politely, but firmly, dismissed.

'. . . Well, thank you for being so frank with me, Mrs Boswell,' he said. 'I'm glad to know she is in such good hands.' He nodded to Dr Mayes and rose. 'I apologise for taking up so much of your time. Do forgive me.'

And still smiling, he left.

Faye sighed. It had been an outwardly peaceful interview but there were strong undercurrents. She turned to Peter Mayes.

'You were right,' she said. 'He is a tricky customer.'

'And it's all being done I imagine, to influence the jury, who will have read the newspapers and the way she is playing it, there is very little we can do about it.'

'Except,' said Peter Mayes, 'to find out why she is losing weight.'

CHAPTER SIXTEEN

The next morning Faye, alone in her house, had no appetite for breakfast, for she had read the morning papers.

'Mary Kyle loses weight' shrieked a black banner headline, and below "My officers don't care, says Governor. Discipline comes first." Then followed a distorted description of her interview with the lawyer. Even *The Times* carried it, though not on the front page – "Lawyer's concern over Miss Kyle" it said.

When she got to her office, Faye asked Radley to take Disciplinary for her and then to come and see her. When he arrived she was speaking to Penny, who had rung to say that the press were on the outside line.

'I'm not available for comment. Any further statements will be issued by the Press Office. Be very firm.'

She rang off and looked at Charles.

'They've got hold of Peter Mayes' home number,' he said. 'They've been ringing him most of the night.'

'Thank heavens I'm ex-directory,' said Faye and then reflected that she had not much else to thank heaven for on this particular morning.

'The newspapers!' she said to Radley, pointing to her desk where they lay.

He picked one up. 'They're only a rehash of the evenings but they've made it sound pretty lurid. What did you really say?'

'I certainly didn't say all those things. The whole conversation is twisted and out of context. And of course I'm not allowed to reply to this. I hope the staff know why I can't defend them in print.'

'They do. Mrs Armitage has explained to them all.'

'Mrs Armitage?' Faye was amazed.

'Peter Mayes spoke to her last night.'

'Well!' said Faye, and thought that here was an unexpected ally.

Then she said seriously, 'I may be in trouble, Charles.'

'I'm afraid you may be,' he answered, and wished he had been present at the interview with the lawyer.

The extension rang. It was Penny.

'I told you to say I was not available,' Faye said and then listened to what Penny had to say, looking, Radley thought, surprised and faintly alarmed.

'Victor Hartnoll?' she repeated.

Radley raised his eyebrows. Victor Hartnoll was a back bencher who saw himself as a thorn in the Government's side and a guardian of the nation's conscience. He was a champion of unpopular causes. He found the publicity he always obtained some compensation for a lack of office. Radley considered him to be a dangerous man.

Faye was still talking to Penny.

'Yes, I'll speak to him . . . Good day Mr Hartnoll, I agree, it's most unfortunate . . . of course you can see her, any day, but not in the morning, I am never free then . . . Very well, I'll wait to hear from you.' She rang off.

'We might have known he'd be the first to get into the act, said Radley.

'I wish he'd kept out,' said Faye. 'But why? Surely he doesn't support the kind of violent anarchy that Mary represents?'

'No, but he's made his reputation as the champion of the underdog. And he can smell national Press coverage.'

'I suspected this was an attempt to win public sympathy for Kyle,' said Faye. 'But I didn't think I would let myself be used so easily.'

'It could have happened to anyone. In a way I feel it is my fault.'

'Nonsense,' said Faye briskly. 'I accept full responsibility for what I said to Stenhill. You weren't even present.'

'I think you'll find everyone will support you.' Radley tried to sound reassuring.

'Do they realise that if her condition does not improve, there may have to be an inquiry?'

'Yes, they're prepared for that. What are you going to do now?'

'About Mary Kyle? Certainly not make any more statements. I'm leaving her to the doctors now. I have other things to get on with. And the first is to see whether I can persuade Chef to change his mind.'

She spoke lightly; then her mood changed and she got up. She looked at Charles Radley.

'If I tell you something, will you treat it with the utmost confidence?' she asked gravely.

'Of course.'

'A friend of mine at the Home Office rang me at home last night – unofficially. I told him I'd been completely misrepresented in the evening paper. He believed me, but he wasn't very reassuring. Our masters are not amused.'

'My dear Faye, this must be absolute hell for you!' said Radley.

'Don't exaggerate, Charles. But I must confess, I wish it hadn't happened.'

When the Governor went up to North Wing after her lunch, she noticed old Mrs Weekes sitting uncomfortably on a hard chair at a small table. When she saw Faye she smiled in a sheepish way, and started to get up, but Faye motioned her to stay sitting and herself sat down at the table.

'Well Mrs Weekes,' she said, 'I'm sorry about this.'

'Yes M'm. It was silly of me.'

'You weren't short of money, were you?'

'No M'm. I don't know what came over me. It was a dress for my sister's grand-daughter. Such a sweet little kiddie. I hadn't took me purse with me.'

'You could have gone back for it next day.'

'Yes'm. It seemed easier to nick it somehow.'

Faye realised that it was a waste of time and effort

to try and talk sense into Mrs Weekes. She was incorrigible. Instead she said,

'What do you think of our improvements here? A lovely wide room isn't it?'

'Oh yes'm,' agreed Mrs Weekes politely. And added, 'Of course I liked it best as it was. But then I'm old fashioned. Pity the uniforms have gone too. Proper mess a lot of these girls look, don't they?'

Faye managed to summon up a wry smile and left Mrs Weekes. She went to have a word with Janet Harker, who exclaimed like everyone else at how well Faye was looking after her holiday. Holiday! thought Faye, it seemed a thousand years ago. They chatted about the Wing generally and Faye, seeing Lily Hever sitting looking sulky in one of the few comfortable chairs, asked how she was behaving.

'She is in a very foul temper,' said Janet. 'I almost wish she'd stayed in her cell. She's upset because old Georgie Weekes will have nothing to do with her.'

'The extraordinary thing about Lily is that she always wants to be "the most popular girl in the dorm" and does absolutely nothing to make herself so,' said Faye. 'I hope it doesn't show, but I have never been able to forgive her for what she did to Norah. I suppose I had better go and have a chat with her just to show willing.'

But Faye was to be spared this particular duty for, as she rose, the telephone in the office rang and Janet Harker answered.

'Assistant Governor North Wing,' she said, and then, 'Yes, she's here.' She passed the receiver to Faye, saying, 'For you, Mrs Boswell. The Deputy.'

'Hullo,' said Radley's voice. 'Victor Hartnoll is at the Gate asking for you.'

'Already?' asked Faye, 'I thought he was going to ring up. Never mind, let's get it over. I'll come to my office now – will you go and escort him up.'

She rang off and turning to Janet told her to ring Mrs

Armitage and to ask her to bring Mary Kyle to her office to meet Mr Hartnoll.

'Victor Hartnoll, the M.P.? I heard he was interested in this case.'

'It's unofficial, Janet.'

'Of course. I hope it goes well,' said Janet, and added warmly, 'He couldn't possibly believe those things you were supposed to have said. No-one who knows you could. Any of us could have told him.'

Faye was touched by her staff's loyalty. First Mrs Armitage, and now Janet.

'Thank you, Janet,' she said. 'I mustn't discuss it, but I do appreciate your faith in me. Now ring the Chief quickly. I mustn't keep the gentleman waiting.'

Victor Hartnoll was a bluff, genial man in his fifties. He wore slightly flamboyant, well-cut clothes. He might have been a prosperous bookmaker. He was a man of great superficial charm and had a following from his many television appearances.

He came in with a flourish, followed by a somewhat dour looking Charles Radley.

'My dear Mrs Boswell! Very good of you to see me at such short notice.'

'I must confess I wasn't really expecting you this afternoon, Mr Hartnoll.' Faye was cool in her manner.

Hartnoll was still smiling.

'If a thing's worth doing, it's worth doing at once. I'm sure none of us wants this affair to get out of hand.'

'No.'

'Of course, I checked with the Home Office before calling you.'

'Of course,' said Faye.

Victor Hartnoll smiled. He realised that Faye intended to play it by the book. Radley felt it time to intervene.

'Mary Kyle's on her way,' he said.

'Good.' The M.P. turned to the Governor. 'Perhaps I could have a word with you before she arrives?'

Faye looked at Radley, who got her message and turned to the door.

'Thank you, Mr Radley,' the Member said graciously.

Radley grunted and left, muttering something about the Works Officer. He hated leaving Faye alone with this particular protagonist.

Victor Hartnoll turned towards Faye with one of his smiles.

'You realise that my visit is entirely unofficial, Mrs Boswell?'

'Yes, I do.'

'I am here purely in my capacity as a private Member of Parliament. Anything you may tell me will be treated as confidential.'

'I'm afraid I have nothing to say, Mr Hartnoll.'

'I gather from my informant at the Home Office, that you already feel you have been misrepresented.' He was still smiling.

'Yes, I do,' said Faye, who had never felt less like smiling.

Victor Hartnoll seemed to find this amusing.

'That can happen to anyone in public life. It's happened to me, constantly. But I have been asked by Mary Kyle's solicitor, and other people acting on her behalf, to look into her treatment, and to see if there is any cause for concern.'

'Yes. I understand,' said Faye, who understood only too well.

'Are you aware of any such cause? He had stopped smiling.

'None at all.' In which she knew she was speaking less that the truth. But what else could she say?

'I see. We are dealing with a potentially explosive situation, Mrs Boswell . . . Many people may see fit to champion her, losing sight altogether of the reason why she is here. It is a case in which justice must not only be done, but be seen to be done. May I see her alone?'

Now we come to it, thought Faye.

'I'm afraid that won't be possible,' she said firmly. I have to be present and send a report of what is said to the Home Office.'

'A pity. This meeting will be useless unless she can speak freely without fear of contradiction.'

'Don't worry. I am here merely as an observer. I cannot speak unless I am asked a direct question.'

'Good,' said Victor Hartnoll.

There was a knock at the door. Faye rose.

'Perhaps you'd like to take my seat. I'll sit here, out of the way.'

'Thank you.'

Victor Hartnoll moved to Faye's seat behind the desk.

'Come in,' said Faye and moved to a seat out of the limelight.

The door opened and Mrs Armitage showed in Mary Kyle. Faye nodded to Mrs Armitage who went out again, closing the door. Mary Kyle stood facing the desk. She glanced from Hartnoll to Faye and back to Hartnoll. She looked grey and unhealthy, with dark circles under her eyes. She walked unsteadily.

'Mary, this is Mr Hartnoll,' said Faye.

Victor Hartnoll rose.

'Do please sit down, Miss Kyle. Now, first of all – do you know who I am?'

'Yes,' said Mary. She sounded wary.

'I am going to ask you some questions and I want you to know you are absolutely free to answer. Is that correct, Mrs Boswell?'

'Quite correct,' said Faye.

'Your solicitor has made a complaint about the way you have been treated while you have been on remand here. Is there anything you want to tell me?'

Mary nodded but said nothing.

'You have lost a considerable amount of weight?'

'. . . Yes,' said Mary.

'Are you receiving medical attention?'

'Since yesterday. Vitamins and pills.'

She was beginning to realise how to play it and the advantage she had in Faye being unable to interrupt.

'Now that interests me. Why was nothing done till yesterday?'

'It was only yesterday Mr Stenhill insisted they looked after me,' Mary said.

Faye was on tenterhooks. What was the girl going to say?

'Surely you were examined by the medical staff before that? Didn't they notice anything?' Victor Hartnoll asked her.

'They said I wasn't worth bothering about.' Mary sounded pathetic. Faye restrained herself with difficulty. This was quite untrue.

'Did you speak to anyone? Did you tell the Governor?' Mary nodded. She glanced quickly at Faye, as if afraid of her.

'What did she say?'

'She said I'd be disciplined if I caused trouble,' answered Mary very quietly.

Hartnoll glanced at Faye, who was staring at Mary Kyle.

She realised the unfair disadvantage she was under. The performance of Mary Kyle as a gentle, browbeaten girl was so very different from her real contemptuous, defiant self.

'She said if I wasn't careful I'd be put on a diet,' Mary added, in a breaking voice.

It was very effective. Mr Hartnoll was beginning to feel really troubled over the girl.

'You have been eating?' he asked, concerned.

'Whatever I can get. But it's terrible. You can hardly swallow it.'

Hartnoll looked at Faye.

'Mrs Boswell, what have you to say to that?'

'Prisoners on remand can have their own food sent in from outside if they ask for it,' said Faye tensely.

'Did you know that?' the M.P. asked Mary.

'I did ask!' answered the girl. 'But they told me what I'd get if I made extra work for them.'

'Who?'

'The screws – the warders,' said Mary.

'You mean they threatened you?'

'Yes. They're always telling me what they'll do if I'm convicted.'

'What will they do?'

'Make me wish I'd been hanged! But it couldn't be worse than it is now. Shouting at me – banging on the door all night to keep me awake . .'

Again Victor Hartnoll looked at Faye. He was not smiling now.

'Are you aware of this, Mrs Boswell?' he asked.

'No. And I do not believe it.' She was finding it hard to control her anger.

'You don't believe it because you don't want to!' Mary was suddenly crying. 'You never see anything. Pulling at me, kicking! Who do you think did this?'

She pulled up her sleeves. On both her arms were lurid bruises, the skin purple and broken. She showed her leg, very thin and badly marked. Faye was horrified. She was certain none of her officers would have done this to the girl. There was a moment's silence. Then Victor Hartnoll rose. He did not speak. Faye pressed the call button on the desk. Mary was still weeping, uncontrollably. A prison officer came in, and led her from the room, supporting her as she swayed.

'What a clever performance,' thought Faye. For she did not believe a word of Mary's story.

But Victor Hartnoll watched her leave and then turned to the Governor.

'These are serious allegations,' he said. 'I think the prison has a case to answer.'

And without a further word, he left.

After he had left Faye with Hartnoll and the prisoner, Radley made his way to the Centre, on his way to the

Remand Wing. He wanted to have a word with the officer in charge. He first told Penny that she was on no account to disturb Faye, not even, he said, 'for the Home Secretary himself.' Penny was looking disturbed over the whole thing.

'It's awful for Mrs Boswell, isn't it sir?' she said and Radley reflected that if it did nothing else, this episode would, at least, prove to Faye that she had, during her eighteen months at Stone Park, earned the affection and respect of her staff.

He himself felt guilty, as Faye herself had been away since soon after the girl was admitted. If it came to a real showdown, he would have to be prepared to take the rap himself, though he knew Faye as Governor would be held responsible. He had reached the Centre and saw Miss Flaxton coming towards him. She seemed agitated.

'Oh sir,' she said. 'Could you possibly come up to North Wing. It's the Chief and Miss Harker. They're having a disagreement.' And she added, 'About a matchbox.'

As Radley went upstairs, he reflected that he could have done without this trivial sort of quarrel today. But, of course, nearly all the uproars in prison were caused by trivia. The Mary Kyle affair was an exception.

When he arrived, the women were standing in groups, listening avidly, as Mrs Armitage, rather red in the face, and Janet Harker, very pale, were confronting each other in her office.

'Now,' said Radley, What's all this about a match box?'

'Lily Hever stole it from Mrs Weekes,' said the Chief shortly.

'And Mrs Armitage forced her to produce it and put her on Report.' Janet sounded heated.

'Of course I did. She'd been stealing,' said the Chief.

'It was so trivial,' retorted Janet. 'I could have dealt with it myself. It is my Wing.' She was annoyed.

From the landing could be heard Mrs Weekes, shrill voice. 'She took my new box of matches. She stole 'em,' and Lily's deeper voice, 'I never, you old bag.'

Radley lost his temper. He felt suddenly impatient with these women. A first-class scandal was blowing up which would affect the officers as much as anyone else, and here they were fighting over a match box. Shortly, and concisely, he told them what he thought and left. He sometimes wished he had never left Cricklewood Prison where he had worked for ten years.

There was silence for a moment after he left, then Janet said, 'He's quite right, of course. I'm sorry Chief.'

Mrs Armitage too grunted an apology. 'All the same,' she added obstinately, 'I'm putting Lily Hever on the charge sheet.'

As soon as she was alone Faye rang Peter Mayes and told him about the bruising. He said he would see the girl at once. He sounded a little disbelieving, as though he thought Fay was exaggerating. She told him, angrily, to go and see for himself and rang off, thinking that tempers were beginning to run too high at Stone Park. Fortunately Mr Morton appeared for one of his sessions, this time longer than usual since the Governor had been away. It lasted for nearly two hours, but the sheer boredom had a calming effect.

As soon as he left, Mrs Armitage came in. She was infuriated by the story of Mary's injuries and reiterated over and over again:

'She did it herself, madam. She did it herself.'

'But it must have caused her tremendous pain,' said Faye.

'She wouldn't mind that. She's tough, that one.' There was a certain grudging admiration in the Chief's voice. 'Besides,' she continued, 'in view of the trouble you're in madam, there's not an officer here who would add to it by striking that particular prisoner at this particular moment. Not that they would ever do so,' she added quickly.

A knock at the door and Peter Mayes came in.

'About that bruising,' he said. 'It looks bad, but it is

neither deep not extensive. Apart from one contused wound on the back of her right leg, and another behind her left shoulder, they look more than they are. One thing is certain – they are all quite recent.'

'Are you sure of that?' asked Faye.

'Positive. I examined her very fully yesterday. Nothing was apparent then.'

Mrs Armitage could bear it no longer.

'They were self-inflicted,' she burst out.

'Could they have been?' Faye asked.

'It's possible. But if they were, she would have to be capable of great determination and ability to stand pain.'

'She's capable of anything,' retorted the Chief.

'What about the loss of weight?' said Faye.

'I'm afraid it's accelerating. As you know, she's permanently in the Hospital Wing and Sister checks to make sure she's eating – but it still continues. All the tests I took have proved to be negative. I must admit to being flummoxed.' He rose. 'Will you look in and see her?' he asked Faye.

'I suppose I'd better,' said Faye. When the doctor had left, Mrs Armitage said to Faye, 'I'm sorry madam. It's all such a shock. If only we had investigated ourselves. We should have put a twenty-four watch on her. I did ask for it.'

'And you were refused?'

'Yes. Mr Radley as good as said I was fussing over nothing, whilst you were away.'

'Oh Charles!' thought Faye. 'You idiot.' Aloud she said, 'No doubt there are many things we could have done. Now we must make sure that nothing else happens and that the staff is completely cleared.'

'Thank you Mrs Boswell.' Faye could hardly believe it, but the Chief sounded grateful. After she had left, Faye sat trying to collect her thoughts, which were whirling. She could imagine what Victor Hartnoll had said to the waiting reporters – he hadn't left until nearly five so it would be too late for the evening papers, though it would make the television news. She must see that the television sets were locked for the early news – it would cause grumbling and discontent, but once it was over the inmates could go back to normal with 'Crossroads' and mercifully, by the time the later news came on, they were all locked up for the night. She checked herself – she was always campaigning for longer hours of freedom. She felt ashamed of her thoughts and said as much to Radley who came in with some memos for the Magistrates' meeting which he wanted her to sign. He told her briefly not to be a fool. She was surprised at his manner.

'Charles!' she said, 'you sound most unlike yourself.'

'I feel it,' he said shortly.

'You need your holiday,' said Faye. 'Where have you and Beth arranged to go?'

Radley's smile was ironic. 'We were going to settle that tonight – have a jolly evening at it. The thing is that at the moment I could not care less.'

'Poor Beth,' thought Faye and said, 'Be prepared for the worst tomorrow. The papers are going to make a meal of this.'

'You're telling me. Try not to worry too much. Tell Bill to take you to a movie.'

'Bill's away,' answered Faye.

'That's too bad. Come and have supper with us – you shouldn't be alone tonight.' For Radley knew that Paul was away.

Faye shook her head.

'You go home and settle your holiday. The one you need so badly.'

CHAPTER SEVENTEEN

Beth Radley was waiting for Charles to return. On the table was a sheaf of travel folders. Tonight, she hoped, was going to be a milestone in their not-so-satisfactory marriage. For the first time for years, instead of an economical holiday staying with his parents near Leeds, or with hers in Devonshire, they had decided to have a real holiday, preferably somewhere in the sun. She felt sure the sun was what Charles needed, sun and a chance to relax; to swim and to go for long walks. Faye had insisted that he took three weeks holiday.

'In a job like ours,' she had said one night when she and Bill came to supper with the Radleys, 'one needs a week to unwind before one can begin to benefit from the holiday': and Charles had reluctantly agreed.

During the past year Beth had grown fond of Faye; they had met for lunch two or three times and Beth often thought that it had been she who had saved their marriage from total collapse. Beth knew that she herself had altered for the worse, her elegant good looks were turning to sharpness, and her manner was becoming brittle and resentful. She was frustrated by her spasmodic sex life and almost as much by their very restricted social life, for she was by nature gregarious. She had almost grown to dislike Charles of late, but believed that a different sort of holiday, where he might be able to forget his work for a few weeks, would help to restore their old relationship.

It was therefore unfortunate that, when Charles did come in, he was unable to talk about anything except the Mary Kyle affair.

'God knows what will happen,' he said. 'Questions in the House for certain.' He was annoyed that Beth had not heard about it on the news.

'I didn't turn it on,' she said. 'I was looking at these' and she held up the folders.

He looked at them blindly, entirely forgetting the plan for the evening, and continued his saga.

This, thought Beth, was too much. She could appreciate his being worried, but not his inability to think of anything except the prison. Deliberately she tore the folders in half and got up.

'I'm going out,' she said flatly. 'Anne is joining a house party in Corsica. I'll go with her. I'll go and arrange it now. You make your own plans. A conducted tour of Mediterranean prisons, perhaps,' she added with a snap; and left the room, shutting the door with a deliberate bang. Charles realised what he had done. He too had been looking forward to this holiday, though he had been too pre-occupied to say so.

Damn Mary Kyle – damn the whole prison service. He got up and went quickly to the door.

'Beth,' he called. 'Don't go. This is important. We must settle this.'

Beth was in the hall, with her coat on.

'What about Kyle?' she queried.

'To hell with Kyle,' retorted her husband and took her firmly by the elbow and removed her coat.

As Faye drove home, she thought of what she had seen in the Hospital Wing where she had been to visit Mary Kyle. The girl had been in bed, her arms heavily bandaged. She virtually refused to speak to Faye, and looked at her coldly. Outside her room, Faye had talked to the Sister; she was as puzzled as the Doctor was over Mary's condition. She also told Faye that whenever she went near the girl Mary shrank back in an exaggerated way as though Sister was going to hit her. She will soon convince herself that she is being brutalised, thought Faye, as she has already convinced Victor Hartnoll.

Faye was tired and depressed when she reached home. It was a damp, drizzling evening with autumn in the air.

She pushed open the front door with no enthusisiam, and to her amazement heard that the record player was on: and on the table in the hall was Bill's large leather brief-case. Before she could speak, he had came out of the sitting room and put his arm around her shoulder.

'Bill!' she said. 'I thought you had to stay till the end of the week.'

'I happened to see the English papers this morning. Tonight was only social stuff and I thought you might need me more.'

'I do – indeed I do.' She hugged him and then went towards the kitchen. 'I must see about your supper.'

He caught her hand and led her to the sofa.

'I'm seeing about yours – in fact I'm taking you out. But first of all drink this,' he put a glass into her hand.

'And tell me all about it.'

She leant back, thankful for his presence.

'Today's papers are nothing to what tomorrow's will be,' she said, and told him the whole story. She knew that, officially, she should not do so. She also knew that Bill's advice and common sense would help her greatly.

When she had finished, he said, 'I've learnt one thing from being in management – when you're in a tough spot, you must be able to rely on your staff, and trust them. Can you?'

'Yes. Today has shown me how much. But they're all looking to me to find a solution to this problem – and I haven't an idea what to do.'

'Try and relax now,' said Bill. 'That's what you used to tell me, remember? When you scolded me for bringing my troubles home with me.'

'You're right,' said Faye. 'It's not fair on you.'

Bill smiled at her. 'I'm not thinking about me. Come on, old love. Relax.'

Faye felt herself growing less tense. But she insisted on watching the news, and the Victor Hartnoll story for he had, of course granted I.T.N. an interview lost nothing in the telling. When it was over Bill got up and turned the television off.

'Yes,' he said. 'I see. It is bad. And you are certain the girl is lying?'

'Absolutely.'

The telephone rang. Bill answered it and passed it to his wife.

'For you,' he said.

It was one of the Assistant Secretaries of the Prison Department, who was also a member of the Prisons Board, the Board in fact which had appointed Faye. She took the instrument with some trepidation. Bill listened to the brief conversation. Faye was tense again, and who could blame her?

'Yes,' she was saying. 'This afternoon. I understood you knew he was coming to see me . . . Yes. It was substantially what I said, but out of context. I've sent a report to you and so has Dr Mayes . . . Yes, my Chief Officer is convinced that the girl is lying and I agree . . .' Her voice changed and became more impersonal. 'Yes, sir. Of course, if you say so. Five o'clock. Yes.'

She rang off and sat in silence for a moment. Then she looked up at Bill.

'I have to go to the Home Office tomorrow afternoon. I'm for it Bill. He didn't sound pleased with me. Never mind. If they sack me, I'll be able to give more time to my neglected husband.' She essayed a smile. Rather a lop-sided one. Faye was not a woman who wept easily but that evening she was near to it. And Bill was not surprised.

From the chimney piece her two children regarded her, Paul who was now living his own life and Virginia who was only a poignant memory. 'Thank heavens I have Bill,' she thought and tightened her grip on his hand.

The next morning it seemed to Faye that a pall hung over Stone Park. The man at the gate did not wear his usual wide grin, the prisoners she passed turned almost furtively away, Peter Mayes looked tired and worried.

Only Mrs Armitage seemed her usual imperturbable self.

'She's twice the woman I am,' thought Faye. She should be Governor.' And realised what a reactionary one she would have been. From the Hospital Wing came the news that Mary Kyle had eaten a good breakfast, but was not looking well. The bruises were beginning to subside, but were still very angry.

At Disciplinary, Faye had to concentrate hard. Her mind kept going back to the headlines in the papers and to her appointment at five o'clock that afternoon. She did not believe she would be able to keep her position as Governor. How could she, a woman who can't control her staff? She listened to requests, handed out reprimands, wondering all the time how much longer she would be sitting in this office in a position of authority.

Mrs Armitage was speaking.

'Lily Hever, madam,' she was saying. With a flourish she laid a small object on the empty space on the desk. Faye looked at it. A box of matches, She remembered now. Surely a trivial offence? In this Faye agreed with Miss Harker. But she must support her Chief Officer. And now here was Lily Hever standing in front of her, smiling in her usual ingratiating way. After Mrs Armitage had described the offence, Lily spoke.

'It was only a box of matches, madam.'

'It's not the value of the object, but the fact that you were caught stealing.'

To Faye's amazement she sounded very cool and professional, despite the turmoil in her mind.

'Give me a chance, madam!' Lily was saying.

'I cannot see how this can fail to affect your remission,' Faye replied.

Lily was in a panic. 'No, madam, wait! If I do you a favour—'

The Chief interrupted, 'You do Madam a favour! Really, Lily!' But Lily was still speaking.

'Look, I'll make a deal. You want to know about Mary

Kyle, don't you? You let me off and I'll tell you what she's up to.'

The Governor and the Chief exchanged glances. Faye heard herself saying coldly.

'I can't make any deals.' She picked up her pen as though about to announce her decision.

Lily was desperate.

'No, listen! The first week she was in here she was sent to the doctor twice for going without food.'

'How did you know that?' asked Faye.

'I was on cleaning in the Remand Wing. And a couple of days later I managed to talk to her, and tipped her off.'

'In what way?'

'I told her, if you don't eat for twenty-four hours, it goes in the Refused Food book, and you go to the doctor. So if you don't want them to stop you, just collect your tray same as usual, then don't eat any, leave a little and get rid of the rest.'

'How?'

'In the toilet of course. All you need is some plastic bags and on remand it's easy to get 'em brought in in magazines. That's the way to go on a hunger strike without anyone knowing. So Mary took my advice. I bet she hasn't eaten a thing. It's weeks now. She looks grey, doesn't she?'

There was silence. Lily Hever – my saviour, Faye was thinking ironically. But she did not show her great relief. Instead she wrote in her book.

'Two days loss of pay and privileges,' she said.

Lily stared at her – had she been believed or not? She was removed. Faye with difficulty restrained herself from embracing Mrs Armitage, her relief was so great. This must be the answer.

'Is she the last?' she asked.

'Yes.'

'Then quickly – up to my office – Dr Mayes – Sister – and Miss Clarke, I think, and of course, yourself. We must act on this, quickly. Lily Hever of all people!'

In the Hospital Wing Mary Kyle had just finished her lunch. Her room was the same size as a cell, with no furnishing, except a small bedside cupboard and a hard chair. In the corner was a washbasin and a lavatory bowl. The walls, thanks to the refurbishing which Faye had sanctioned, were painted a soft pink. There was a curtain over the open door. Mary was wearing a shapeless woollen dressing gown over a nightdress. She was sitting with the nearly empty tray over her knees, as Sister came in.

'So you've finished up,' she remarked brightly. 'Good! Here is the paper you wanted' and she laid a newspaper on the bed. When she had gone, Mary read it avidly. The staring headlines on the front page especially pleased her. She lit a cigarette, and had to put it out almost at once: she was finding it increasingly difficult to smoke; it now caused waves of nausea.

After listening to make sure that all was quiet outside, she rose, feeling very weak. She was holding her side as though she was in pain. When she reached the lavatory, she opened her dressing gown and took out a plastic bag. It was clipped at the top and inside was her entire lunch, in a squashed mess. She opened the bag and shot the contents into the pan. She crumpled up the bag and was about to throw it in too. Suddenly she heard a sound and looked round. The Chief stood there. Grabbing the handle, Mary was about to pull it, and to get rid of the evidence.

But Mrs Armitage was too quick for her.

'No, you don't,' she said, and seized Mary's wrist, and she did not do it gently.

Behind her were the Governor and several others, their faces implacable. Mary was trapped and she knew it.

Feeling almost light-headed with relief, Faye rang the Home Office. Within an hour the message came back. In the circumstances she need not keep her appointment, but they would like a report, as soon as possible. She and Charles Radley spent the afternoon getting it out.

'Make some extra copies, Penny,' ordered Faye. 'I want one to show Mr Hartnoll.'

'You're not going to have the pleasure again?' asked Radley.

'At five o'clock.' Faye chuckled. 'I'm looking forward to it. And this time, Charles, you must be present.' She added, 'Did you and Beth decide on your holiday?'

'Yes. If you don't object, we're going to your hotel. It seemed to have everything.'

'Object? My dear Charles, I am delighted. I'll write and tell Madame Voisin to make a fuss of you both.'

When Victor Hartnoll arrived, full of bombast and uttering implied threats, Faye asked him to read the report before he said anything about the case. He read it in silence. Faye felt he was visibly deflating as he did so. Then he laid the report on the desk.

'So – she's been on a secret hunger strike.'

'Yes,' said Faye.

'Four witnesses, eh? I see. And a Welfare officer! I suppose the bruises were self-inflicted?'

'Yes. They were a smoke-screen. They appeared at just the right time to confuse us.'

Victor Hartnoll nodded. 'It's exceedingly fortunate that this was found out today. I had been going to speak in the House tonight.'

'Had been going to?' asked Faye.

He took her meaning and smiled.

'Well – I may still say a few words.'

'About Mary Kyle?'

'Well – that might be considered a breach of confidence. No, if the Prison Service is brought up, I shall describe the splendid conditions I have found here – and the high state of morale.'

His smile this time was a little patronising. Faye decided to cut him down to size.

'If you speak on the subject at all, Mr Hartnoll, I'd prefer you to describe it as it really is. Depressing, understaffed, with the prisoners in inadequate accommodation.

We have done what we can, and we always will but, until the whole place is rebuilt, we are horribly overcrowded.'

Nonplussed, Victor Hartnoll bowed and left.

Charles, smiling broadly, came towards her.

'You put him in his place,' he said. 'Nevertheless, I hope he doesn't mention Stone Park.'

'He won't,' said Faye. And she was right.

'I'm more glad than I can say that it's all turned out so well,' said Radley, warmly. 'We couldn't have spared you. Congratulations on clearing it up.'

'Don't congratulate me. It's all due to the horrible Lily.'

They both laughed and, shortly after, Radley left.

Faye had a word with the vastly relieved Doctor and made some other necessary calls. She thought with some sympathy of Mary Kyle. She might not spare others but she did not spare herself either. She would probably be a permanent resident at Stone Park after her trial. Faye wished that political prisoners could have separate accommodation. In these troubled days they were increasing all the time and they did not mix well with the other inmates.

A knock on the door and the Chief came in.

'Can I bother you, madam?'

'That's what I'm here for.'

'It's a Mrs Lolos – a Greek lady, on remand. Shoplifting. Very smartly dressed. Plenty of money on her. I can't think why she hasn't got bail.'

'What's the trouble?'

'She's creating mayhem in the remand wing, without a word of English. We wondered—' she paused. . . 'Do you speak Greek, madam?'

'A little,' said Faye, and added with a twinkle, 'Bring her up, Chief.'

NIGEL NICOLSON
PORTRAIT OF A MARRIAGE

Portrait of a Marriage tells the story of Harold Nicolson's forty-nine-year marriage to Vita Sackville-West, a union based on mutual trust, shared interests, deepening love, total frankness and reciprocal infidelity. It is also the journal of Vita's love affair with Violet Trefusis, the crisis which nearly broke the Nicolsons' unconventional, but extraordinarily successful marriage.

'Vita's . . . journal will earn an honoured place in the records of confessional literature.'
THE TIMES

'Excels for intensity and unexpectedness anything of its kind in fiction.'
FINANCIAL TIMES

'Mr Nicolson's good faith is patent . . . the tone perfect.'
Sybille Bedford, THE LISTENER

'THE MOST CONVINCING AND ENTHRALLING OF LOVE STORIES.'
ECONOMIST

MAHLER

Kurt Blaukopf

Mahler: the child prodigy who was composing at the age of four; the musician whose genius anticipated the great era of stereophonic recording; the conductor who revolutionised concert hall and opera house; the man whose symphonies inspired Thomas Mann's DEATH IN VENICE.

Kurt Blaukopf traces the story of Mahler's life and work against its background of the disintegrating Austro-Hungarian Empire, through his relationships with the three women he loved, his battle to win directorship of the Vienna Court Opera to the final breakdown and the crisis of his meeting with Freud a year before his death. An outstanding study of the man whose work is a landmark in twentieth century music.

THE PALLISERS Anthony Trollope

THE PALLISERS

Set amid the swirl of London's social and political life in the 1860's, Anthony Trollope's sequence of six parliamentary novels follows the fortunes of Plantagenet Palliser, dedicated politician, heir to the greatest dukedom in Britain, and his beautiful, extrovert wife, Glencora. Interwoven with their story are those of 'Planty Pall's' colleagues and Glencora's social allies and rivals, from wily Lizzy Eustace, obsessed by her famous family diamonds, to the naif Irishman Phineas Finn and his four loves.

This saga of romance, intrigue, blackmail and even murder, originally amounted to more than a million and a half words, written for leisured Victorian readers. For modern readers Michael Hardwick has produced this single volume edition, skilfully abridged to preserve the spirit and intention of Trollope's great work.